# Blown Away

Books by Ronald Sukenick

*Blown Away*
*The Endless Short Story*
*In Form: Digressions on the Art of Fiction*
*Long Talking Bad Conditions Blues*
*98.6*
*Out*
*The Death of the Novel and other Stories*
*Up*
*Wallace Stevens: Musing the Obscure*

# Blown Away

A Novel by Ronald Sukenick

Sun & Moon Press
Los Angeles

Copyright © Ronald Sukenick, 1986
Cover: "Regard and Abandon," by Robert Yarber
    courtesy Sonnabend Gallery, New York

Publication of this book was made possible, in part, through a grant from the National Endowment for the Arts and through contributions to the Contemporary Arts Educational Project, Inc., a non-profit corporation.

*The New American Fiction Series:* 7

Library of Congress Cataloging in Publication Data

Sukenick, Ronald
        Blown Away
        (New American fiction series 7)
        1. Title   II. Series
PS3569.433B56 1986 813'.54 86-23048
ISBN: 0-940650-63-0
ISBN: 0-940650-64-9 (paper)
ISBN: 0-940650-65-7 (signed cloth)

10    9    8    7    6    5    4    3    2    1
FIRST EDITION

Sun & Moon Press
6363 Wilshire Blvd., Suite 115
Los Angeles, California 90048
(213) 653-6711

*for Julia, my good spirit*
*(& P.K.)*

# I

# VISION

Psychics can see the color of time it's blue. Changes in shade intensity brilliance are important to those of us who are sensitive. Today time is indigo. Indigo is heavy. It condenses in the air of the parlor like a dense cloud descending on the formica table on the crystal ball the cat the tacky couch. I have never seen indigo time that wasn't heavy pregnant foreboding I start. To shake it probably has to do with the moon which. Shakes. Moon in Taurus. Anything could happen but. On the verge. Stomach cramps I. Saturn in Pisces. Cramps. Inhale. Exhale. Inhale . . . exhale . . . inhale . . . exhale . . . one—two—three . . . three—two—one . . . one—two—three . . . three—two—one . . . deeper in . . . deeper out . . . a parting of darkness . . . spring is coming . . . youth and happiness . . . I see a young woman . . . I hear the wind blowing . . . voices . . . she's going to do it till she gets it right . . . bring me back a ham sandwich . . . I see a love affair that plants the seeds of death enjoy it while you can . . . failure . . . drowning . . . a blinding light beyond which . . . nothing . . .

Now it will begin. I am the omniscient narrator. But while most tellers tell a tale already set, I tell tales that haven't happened yet. Reading my own mind I, like a crab, think sideways into the future. I finish my tea glance at the leaves which imply misadventure and in a temper invert the mug. Presto chango. Expresso digresso. It turns to gum. What will happen is I fall in love with a woman young enough to be my daughter she won't be worth it. What will happen is I look into my crystal ball and see my own tomb the epitaph says avoid the future. What will happen is I tell my own fortune the fortune teller. An unfortunately fatal love affair fortunately affords the chance to reclaim my fortune. I see Miracle panic-stricken fighting the Santa Ana winds in his seaplane forced down at Catalina Island, his myth of success reduced to the fact of his fuel gauge. I see Drackenstein in his sloop out of Newport Beach fearfully foundering in the same winds run aground on the same shores. But this coincidence, Leo, is no coincidence. Sometimes you have to sail the wrong way to catch the right wind. As Drackenstein cheated me in business, so Miracle did Drackenstein dispossess. Now the shock of mortality makes everyone contrite, and gives us the chance to set things right. Death narrows the plurality of myth to the singularity of fate. If I act fast I can right old wrongs. And maybe commit some new but what can I tell you. This is what I see. I saw. I have a blind date with fate. But now, my furry friend, I sense Philitis at my door.

What will happen is I open the door on Philitis' startled face as his fist knocks on nothing and he stumbles into my parlor, apologizing profusely with all the aggravating pathos of an Aries with Saturn in the fourth house. As usual in my presence his aura is dull grey and jerky, Saturn in fall to Cancer. He stands there staring at me a flash of pale yellow dots running through the auric pulse like bubbles through alka seltzer.

"Good morning Dr. Ccrab." *You look sick*.

"What do you mean I look sick?"

"I didn't say that."

"I know you didn't say it, I want to know what you mean by it."

"You're pale." *You smell bad*. Philitis turns pinkish.

"It's stuffy, Philitis. Might be better to open the window."

He opens it. The odor is strong obviously, it always coincides with the cramps. Gas and turbulence. For Cancers the stomach is a way of knowing, a painful epistemology. The price of prophecy.

"Sit down Philitis. How are the rats?"

"I told you I don't work with rats anymore Dr. Ccrab."

"That's right I keep forgetting. You work with me."

Philitis sits down on my tacky couch, which creaks irately. The cat, Leo, jumps down from the formica table with a thump and stalks into a corner where he curls himself up into an immense black furball, white paws and drooping whiskers protruding. Blond, quite young, face like Botticelli's Primavera.

"About nineteen years old."

"Who? What?"

"I see a fish."

"I'm not following you Dr. Ccrab."

"What do I know about Hollywood?"

"Are you going to Hollywood?"

"I'm going to Westwood. To your class, let's go." I catch myself in the mirror as I get up, greying, balding, bellying, middle-aging. A nineteen year old this time, here we go again. "Only yesterday I was making plans Philitis, plotting the future. But the future has its own plot in which our own petty scenarios are often lost."

"Do you mind if I turn the recorder on Dr. Ccrab?"

"Why not, that's what you're paying for. You didn't bring the check today?"

"My office sent a note saying you should have it soon."

"Life is not a fortune cookie. My clairvoyant intuition tells me we're going to stop at your office."

"After class."

"Before class." I bend down to pet Leo. What is this thing I have with women? Moon rules Cancer. It always leads to trouble, to the unpredictable, the attraction of knowledge for the unknown, of the seer for the unforeseen, of the fortunate for misfortune, of life for death, of fire for air. And yet my ambition is to be utterly conventional, normal, predictable. Adversity is in the I of the beholder. I can feel my eye trouble coming on. The room shimmers and goes blank, what will happen is I'll go see Wang, Philitis disappears. Sight fails, vision amplifies. Expresso digresso. I am reading a letter in an ancient script that I don't understand. It reveals I have the same fingerprints as the scriptural Egyptian trying to insert the living heart in the golden calf. But the golden calf has no heart. This is a message from elsewhere. Everything keeps coming back to the same message a message I don't want to read. The scene changes again. Expresso digresso. Bring me back a ham sandwich. A love affair. An obscure saloon, tobacco smoke, beer smell.

"You don't say hello?"

"I'm doing a form," Wang will say, staring intensely at a point in front of his face. To the ordinary person it would appear that Dong Wang is slouched over the bar of The Fat Black Pussy Cat in his tacky Hawaiian shirt a cigar butt hung in his fingers drinking a beer. But as I should have noticed he is actually going through a long complicated T'ai Chi form without lifting a finger. As a mind reader I am one of the few people if not the only person who can appreciate this performance. I always enjoy it in fact it always has a strangely beneficial effect on me. Stroking the Peacock's Tail, White Crane Exposes Wing. I especially appreciate today his strong graceful execution of Step Back and Repulse the Monkey. Wang, who is a squat, pock-faced, middle-aged Oriental, gives no outward indication of his activity other than the strenuous heaving of his fat belly from which his cobalt aura pulses in a blaze that envelops his whole body in a fluctuating teardrop of rays and brilliance. With his greasy hair hanging down over his face and his eyes bugging with effort he looks like some kind of Mongoloid lunatic, a look that's worth bucks to him as a character actor in horror films and Kung Fu awful awfuls. He continues concentrating for a few moments, then slumps on the stool and gulps his beer as the auric pulse subsides. "How do you do that?" I ask him.

"You use your imagination. Same way you read minds."

"I had a vision, Dong."

"What did you see?"

"My grave. I'm going to die."

"We're all going to die. It's our fate. Fate is always fatal. What else?"

"A girl. A love affair. A lot of grief, complications, adventures."

"What is this thing you have with women?"

"The moon rules Cancer."

"Be careful with this girl. And don't talk about death. Talking seals your fate. You may have had a vision but precognition is one thing and superstition is another. You never know about the truth of precognition till after the fact. So why get melodramatic? What else?"

"I'm going to get the chance to call Drackenstein to account."

"Are you still chewing that over? Forget the money. It's ancient history. Let it go."

"It's not only the money. It's that I don't want to concede the injustice. It's a question of whether we consent to live in a moral world or an immoral one."

Wang laughs, gets up moving like a cat. Dong Wang isn't his real name. Ccrab isn't my real name either. He stretches and shakes himself.

"Do you have the fortunes?" he asks.

Every week for a certain sum I do the fortunes for Wang's cookie factory. If you get one of Dong Wang's fortune cookies you know you're getting the real thing. He takes the envelope and opens it, reading down the sheet of paper. " 'You will soon embark on a voyage.' Um. 'Soon, and with somebody pleasant.' Provocative. 'Worldly failure leads to real success.' Isn't that a little dull?"

"The truth is often dull."

"My customers don't want the truth. They want something they can talk about, a conversation piece. I keep telling you that Ccrab."

"I can't help it."

" 'You will soon have another oriental meal.' I like that. It's good for business. Speaking of business . . ." Wang pays the bartender and we walk out on Broadway into the hazy Los Angeles sun. I stop at an Oriental foodstand for a burrito, then we stroll down to Wang's storefront on Sunset: KARMIC KOOKIE KOMPANY.

"Watch out for Drackenstein," says Wang. "He who grasps the bull by the horns will sometimes find he has the tiger by the tail. That's what the man says."

"The man has a terrible addiction to cliché."

"What would we do without cliché? How would we communicate our insights?"

"I don't know, but life is not a fortune cookie. My clairvoyant intuition tells me we're going to stop at your office."

"After class."

"Before class."

"Dr. Ccrab?" *Is he in a trance?*

Philitis is disturbed because I'm frozen bent over Leo. "I meant to pet him. I forgot," I explain. I pet him.

"We'll take my car?" Philitis says hopefully.

"You know better than that. We'll take my Plumyth."

The Plumyth makes Philitis nervous, he always thinks it's going to break down on the freeway. Personally I'm indifferent to cars as long as they don't go too fast, and if there's one thing that's sure about the Plumyth it won't go too fast. An old whale with huge tail fins and the brand name knocked off in some accident put back in the wrong order missing an o. The Plumyth is parked on Hyperion near De Longpré in front of my sign: DR. BORIS O. CCRAB, and on a shingle below, MENTIST. The shingle is a leftover from the bungalow's previous tenant, a dentist. Instead of throwing it away, I have the thrifty idea of changing the d to an m, incidentally inventing a new profession. My ingenuity is oddly echoed by the ingenuousness of the real estate agent across the Avenue whose sign, long in disrepair, reads: GOLDEN STATE REAL OR.

I leave the bungalow unlocked, nothing to steal, and we go down the several sets of stairs, first through orange, lemon, grapefruit, and avocado trees more or less wild, then, on the lower terraces, star jasmine, bird-of-paradise, prickly pear, red hot poker, bottle brush, fuchsia, bougainvillea, oceanothus and crustacean ice plant growing down to the sidewalk with its pink and violet flowers. Leo follows us down the stairs except, not wanting to appear doggish, pretends not to follow. Every time I look at him he sidles off in another direction: *Who me? I'm not even here, I'm just sniffing this flower.* The cat sees himself being seen. But can he see himself seeing? Can you read your own mind? Can consciousness understand itself? That's the philosopher's stone, the rosetta stone, whose mysterious language carries its own decodification, the myth that includes its demythification.

Philitis looks at the Plumyth as if it were going to attack him.

"Let me untie the front door for you," I offer Philitis out of politeness.

"That's all right Dr. Ccrab," he says glumly. "I'll get in your side. Did you get your glasses yet?"

"You don't need glasses if you don't drive too fast."

Leo gets in the back. After the first two efforts of the starter Philitis is already discouraged. "Does it have gas?"

"I don't know, the gauge is broken. But as with many things you often have to try three times. That is one of my many minimyths. It often works."

"And if it doesn't?"

"I call the garage."

On the third try the Plumyth starts. I get on the Hollywood Freeway at Vermont to avoid the local traffic: Hollywood Freeway—Harbor Freeway—Santa Monica Freeway—San Diego Freeway. It's a crisp clear day of the kind we still get here now and then like a gift from the gods, the hills off to the left like enchanted ramparts, today even the snowpeaks beyond Pasadena glitter above the balmy city. Like Los Angeles thirty years ago. Some fairytale combination of Rome, Mexico City, China. I always enjoy breezing along the freeways in the old Plumyth at forty miles an hour or more when the traffic is light. Philitis turns his recorder on. Leo goes to sleep in the back. Flashing red lights in the rearview mirror. I pull over and stop. A tough looking Highway Patrol officer pokes his face into the window.

"You know how fast you were going mister?"

"I wasn't speeding."

"Take a guess."

"Forty?"

"Twenty-five miles an hour. You know this is a very interesting vehicle you got here. You got a cracked windshield, at least two bald tires, two broken tail lights and your tail pipe is smoking like the *Queen Mary*. Don't you believe in ecology? And what's all that rope on the door?"

"The latch doesn't work."

The officer takes out his ticket book. "This is going to take a while," he says. At this point Leo jumps onto my shoulder from the back seat. "What's that," says the officer. "No animals obstructing the driver, that's another violation."

Leo lets out a piercing howl.

"Jesus," says the officer. "What kind of a huge cat is that?" He makes the mistake of looking into Leo's eyes.

"This is a very interesting cat, officer. He is known as a Nepalese. They have the reputation of being extremely intelligent, officer. If you will notice his eyes, officer, you will see that they have a very, very intelligent expression. In Nepal and Tibet they say that when a man dies his soul, for a time, takes up residence in these cats. They also say that when a man is going to die such cats will sometimes begin to look like him, and that is how you know a man is going to die. Does he look like anyone you know, officer? This particular animal is from Katmandu, officer. The cats of Katmandu are considered holy animals, officer. Katmandu is a wonderful city, officer. Wouldn't you like to visit Katmandu? In Katmandu everyone is extremely helpful and friendly. In Katmandu everyone is extremely helpful and friendly. In Katmandu when someone is not extremely helpful and friendly all you have to do is clap your hands and they become extremely helpful and friendly. Extremely helpful and friendly. In a second I am going to clap my hands." I clap my hands.

The officer is staring into Leo's blinkless eyes, fascinated, his face blank. "Well that's quite a cat you got there," says the officer. "Quite a cat. I've always liked a nice cat." He reaches out to pet Leo, who allows himself to be petted. "Nice pussycat. Good pussypuss. By the way you have a lot of violations on this vehicle. This is a dangerous vehicle. If I were you I'd get some of the violations repaired on this vehicle. In fact if I were you I'd probably drive this vehicle into a junkyard and leave it there. You'd probably live longer, know what I mean. I want you to promise me you'll get these violations repaired."

"I promise, officer."

"Good. That's what I like to hear. You can go ahead now."

"Thank you, officer."

"And sir."

"Yes, officer?"

"Have a nice day."

I pull out, Leo still perched on my shoulder. I glance over at Philitis. He looks completely freaked out.

"Did you get that on your tape Philitis?"

"Yes I did Dr. Ccrab."

"What did you think?"

"Unreal."

"What makes you so sure what's real and what's unreal? You see something you don't want to believe so you call it unreal. That's your rat psychology training. But on the other hand you may have a point. Maybe it was unreal. Maybe I didn't hypnotize the cop. Maybe I hypnotized you, Philitis. Maybe there never was a cop, Philitis. Maybe you're in a trance right now, Philitis. Maybe you've been in a trance since you walked into my parlor this morning, Philitis. Maybe we're still in my parlor. Maybe this hasn't happened yet. Maybe, Philitis, you've been in a trance since the first time you laid eyes on me. Philitis, look at me. Maybe this is all a prediction and you're just a figment of my imagination. Maybe the present is just the prediction of the future by the past."

"You're doing a number on me, Dr. Ccrab."

"Look at the hills then. Don't they look beautiful today? Don't they look almost too beautiful? Don't they look too beautiful to be real? Maybe they're part of my spell. Or maybe we're both part of some other spell. Maybe the weather itself has cast a spell, maybe the whole city is enchanted today. And maybe not only today. And maybe not only the city. Maybe experience is a number done by nothing on infinity."

"Hold it a minute if you don't mind. I have to change the cassette."

From the Plumyth I can see the giant Hollywood sign, white against the khaki of the hills, which like Hollywood itself has been allowed to degenerate till now it's missing an l. Expresso digresso. I can see myself lecturing to Philitis' class, sitting at the desk, Leo on my shoulder, the students in this small lecture hall assiduously taking notes while I try to reduce everything sufficiently to cliché.

"Now you are wondering, after observing these admittedly petty demonstrations, how I get a cat to read minds, predict the throw of the dice and decipher your past from the way you pet him. Even Professor Philitis here is skeptical. Many of you suspect a trick—you there, in the back row left, for example. Well, you're right. There is a trick. And here it is."

I take the can of tuna fish and can opener from my battered briefcase and open the can. "I'm too smart to try to get away with something in front of a class of parapsychology students. The trick is not only to receive information from and transmit suggestions to Leo, but simultaneously telepathize to him the promise of a can of tuna fish."

I set the open can on the desk and Leo, jumping down, eagerly starts eating.

"We're all familiar with animal behavior Dr. Ccrab. What's your explanation of the powers involved? How does this work?" asks Philitis.

"I don't explain it I just do it and it just works. If I explained it you wouldn't understand anyway. Time is a substance I've told you this before. Its visual manifestation is light. That's why nothing is faster than the speed of light. When through intense concentration you make time more dense it becomes a medium of communication and finally an actual physical force. In the ordinary time-field effect usually occurs later than cause. So we have motivation, plot, narrative, the Old Testament, Greek ontology, in short, history. In the dense psychic time-field cause occurs simultaneously with effect, which is to say there are no causes and effects. Everything is simultaneous. Contained in the book of eternity. Already written. Nothing happens. Or everything happens. This is what we call unification. In a weakly unified field, as in our world, most things happen in order some things happen out of order. In a perfectly unified field there would be no such thing as order. Everything would be interconnected. One vast coincidence. Everything would be part of everything else. Think sideways. Astrology, precognition, fortune telling. Time is because we can't take everything in at once. It is not even impossible that in the cosmos at its most creative, effect occurs before cause, so that only analytic retrospect can rationalize the synthetic event which will already have happened in the future, or even that some things happen without cause. That's why events are always more evident than their causes, and why the only thing that's perfectly clear is what hasn't happened yet."

"I don't completely follow you Dr. Ccrab," says Philitis. "You see what we're trying to get at is the big idea behind psychic phenomena. I think there might be a big idea there. A big idea that could change our whole way of looking at things."

"The big idea is not to drown in your own experience. That's been the big idea since men crawled out of the cave. That's the big idea behind the big idea."

Philitis looks at his watch. "I think our session is about over today," he tells the class. "Dr. Ccrab will be back next week."

The class gets up and straggles out. "Excuse me Professor Philitis." Like the sound of crystal or a bell I hear her voice with my whole body. "Is it cool if I sit in on your course?" I don't even turn around. Yet. I wish I had shaved this morning. Or even yesterday morning. Cathy Jane. Joan. June. Fish. I'm already in love. Before first sight. Expresso digresso. Bring me back a ham sandwich.

"Hold it a minute if you don't mind," says Philitis. "I have to change the cassette."

From the Plumyth I can see the giant Hollywood sign white against the khaki of the hills which, like Hollowood itself, has been allowed to degenerate till now it's missing an l. Philitis discovers he's out of cassettes and figures there's no point in talking, so the rest of the drive is restfully vacant. Philitis has a mind like an open book that you don't want to read. Soon we're on the Santa Monica. I amuse myself with the signs on the freeway: Arlington Ave. Crenshaw Blvd. Hail La Brea! Washington Believed. Farewell Fairfax, Ave! Ave! Venice Believed. La Cienega Believed. Why am I going to disorder my life, what's left of it, with another love affair? Control wanes, anything might happen, the more you know the less you know. It's out of order we're shooting out of sequence. Producer-director Rod Drackenstein's shoestring production *My Little Pig* has grossed an amazing eight million dollars in eight weeks and attendance is mounting. I know I can only fulfill my fate through women I know I'm doomed to be restless and subject to constant ebb and flow. Moon in first house. The success of *Pig* has given its young star Clover Bottom instant notoriety. I'm extremely nervous with depression just around the corner. What chaos, what new failures am I about to open myself to. What will she be like. Venus in Scorpio. The planet of beauty rises in the sign of sensual power. Dark spring. I feel like I have a blind date with fate. Expresso digresso. I chew my lip and wait.

"I love order," I tell Wang. Tobacco smoke, beer smell. "I love order like a drowning man loves the land. I plot the order of fate from the planets of fortune. Unfortunately order always leads to doom, that's the secret meaning of tragedy."

What will happen is I meet Dong Wang in The Fat Black Pussy Cat.

"Doom?" says Wang. "Let's not exaggerate. You mean reincarnation. Who said you have to die to be reincarnated? It's probably that young girl you've been fucking. A little reincarnation like that never hurt anyone, especially you. You get too abstract, if you don't look out you're going to vaporize and turn into a theory."

"Do you know the root meaning of theory? Passionate contemplation. That's what I'm into with Cathy June." I pull the pin-up photo of Cathy June out of my wallet, nude with her ass up in the air, and hand it to Wang who vents a whistle. The customer on the next bar stool over tries to get a look.

"Contemplation my ass, you fucking sexist. How did she fall for you?"

"I hypnotized her."

"Prick. Can you hypnotize one for me?" He orders two more beers. I tell him I don't want any.

"They're both for me," he says. "She's going to fuck you up."

"On the contrary, she's going to be a star, and she's going to help me get my money back from Drackenstein. As I will sell her to Drackenstein so Drackenstein will sell her to Miracle."

"Forget it," says Wang. "Your intentions are impure and can only bring you trouble. Your worship of the golden calf always turns out to be a way of sacrificing yourself, that's your karma. You know this. I think you've been going off the deep end lately. You should never have hypnotized this girl. She's not your type. It's part of your ongoing pursuit of vulgarity. You have a taste for tarts. You want your life to be coarse and simple. Like I have a taste for women who are complex and mysterious. The kind I never get or if I get them they turn out to be coarse and simple. That's because I'm crude and stupid."

"You're in a bad mood today."

"I'm thinking about death Boris. I'm thinking about how unexpected it is, how abrupt," says Wang.

"I've already told you you're going to die on July 13, 1996 of massive head injuries. It won't hurt."

"Big help. Besides it's always a surprise. It's always discontinuous. It never fits into the plot."

"It fits into the cemetery plot. That's the only plot it has to fit into."

"Very witty," says Wang. "You're not supposed to have a sense of humor. It doesn't become you. It ruins your style."

"I don't want style," I tell him. "My ambition is to be utterly conventional. Normal. Predictable."

"You're too much in touch with reality to be normal. Death, chaos, and chance are not normal. You're a control freak. And you're too fat. I know you have a double life but it doesn't mean you have nine lives like Leo. Stay away from Taco Bells and Der Wienerschnitzels if you're worried about yourself," Wang advises me.

"I like junk food. I want to incorporate the ordinary."

"Baloney."

What will happen is we stop at Ships in Westwood for lunch before going on campus while I try to explain to Philitis how I discovered Leo's powers.

"One day it struck me that Leo looked a little like Edward G. Robinson. This made no sense to me so naturally I forgot about it, a good example of how people lose their power. By ignoring it. Next day Leo was the spitting image of Edward G. Robinson, that squat, jowly look. That night I heard on the radio Robinson had died. Then Dong Wang told me about the holy cats of Katmandu. Why Robinson chose Leo I have no idea, they weren't acquainted so far as I know. No, Leo is not from Nepal I made that up for the benefit of the cop, he's just a giant furry mutt Persian."

As I sit there popping toast in the toasters provided at each table, Carlos will pass by. He waves without stopping. "I'm in Mexico," he says. Meaning, I presume, he's also in Mexico, visiting Don Juan no doubt. I'd met him chez Anais, another sorceress of sorts. For both Nin and Carlos the medium is language, in my case I myself am the medium. Philitis reverses the cassette and presses record.

"How do you explain this Robinson business Dr. Ccrab?"

"How do I know," I tell him. "Maybe the soul likes to leave the body in good time, like rats and sinking ships. Speaking of Ships, waitress, if this place makes hot fudge sundaes I'd like one. Chocolate. And a hot chocolate. There are a lot of mysteries Philitis."

*He's making this up*, thinks Philitis.

"Not only am I not making it up Philitis but sometimes when somebody is about to die, most often suddenly, Leo will start to look like that person."

"Do you believe in the soul?"

"I don't believe in anything. I believe what I see. I believe in Leo. What are you doing, are you crazy?"

"What? What?" Philitis was about to light his pipe with a match taken from the back row of a fresh matchbook. I snatch the book out of his hand and throw it on the floor. How crazy can you get?

"What did I do?" says Philitis.

"When you start a fresh matchbook begin with a match from the outside row, preferably outside left. What you were about to do is very bad luck."

"Why?"

"Some things are just, how can I put it. Out of order."

"What actually does the 'Dr.' in your title stand for?" asks Philitis a little later.

"M.M.D. Doctor of Mental Medicine. Mentist for short."

We'll be walking across the campus of U.C.L.A., Leo riding on my shoulder creating a stir among the strolling coeds some of whom stop to pet him. One of the pleasant aspects of the campus is that the girls tend to look like starlets, trim, tan, precisely groomed. I take the opportunity to hand out my card:

Dr. Boris O. Ccrab, Mentist

Readings

Astrological Consultant to

The Stars & other Famous People

Syndicated Horoscope Commentator

I invite the prettier ones to come around for a free reading, every now and then one of them will say yes. Not that, as you'll jump to conclude, I'm interested in seduction. I have a very limited appetite for the sensual. Love is something else of course. No, pretty women interest me because they have interesting destinies here. Fish. Venus in Scorpio. Responds to can opener. What does it feel like to have the most famous fanny in Hollywood. Bring me back a ham sandwich. You have an energy break there. Mars in Pisces. I'm really into it. Couldn't wait 4 u 2 call. 2 superspacey. P.S. u wurent hear. Fortuna square Pluto in Cancer. Venus semisextile Uranus from an uncongenial sign. You're my thesis. I did it with time. A little off balance. It was all fake.

"No rats this time Dr. Ccrab," says Philitis.

I discover we're in a lab, in what must be the Psychology Department, which is in fact ratless. I must have forgotten getting there, my old problem of absent mindedness, my mind is absent because it's somewhere else. Philitis' check, I notice, is in my hand. Last time he'd gotten us a lab full of caged white rats that had so distracted Leo he couldn't perform. Today we try again. Philitis is perspiring heavily as we prepare. His aura assumes a jumpy greenish quality. He smells like old meat.

"Let me emphasize I'm already under pressure from my dissertation directors," says Philitis. "You're my thesis. I've staked my career on your psychic powers. If there are any tricks involved in this experiment I wish you'd tell me now."

"Do we have to go through this every time Philitis? Where's the toilet here?"

Philitis glances at me suspiciously. *He just went to the bathroom*, he thinks. *What's he up to?*

"Don't worry Philitis. It's not for me. It's for Leo."

"I see." *Leo uses the toilet?*

"For drinking. He likes to drink from the toilet. Chacun à son gout."

Today's performance consists of transmitting telepathic messages to Leo while Philitis televises the result. For Philitis this is really hot stuff but actually telepathic communication is easier with animals probably because they have less static in their consciousness. There's something particularly pure about Leo's aura, for example, a kind of clear pearly blue what the painters call Paris blue, *bleuâtre*. The problem with Leo isn't transmission but getting him to respond to what's transmitted since as everyone knows cats are extremely independent creatures with ways of their own. The trick then—a trick I conceal from Philitis—is to not only transmit the suggestion but also simultaneously the promise of a can of tuna fish.

However Leo doesn't respond, he's stubborn today. What's the problem? Of course. I forgot the can opener. I not only visualize a can opener, but imagine the sound of a can opener. Leo always responds to the sound of a can opener, and then, furthermore, I picture emptying the can onto a plate. This is too much for Leo. He stretches, gets up, and quickly bats the red ball to all the places required by the experiment. As an added fillip I send the ball rolling back toward Leo through telekinesis. Leo bats it away impatiently. He wants his tuna fish.

Philitis turns off his TV camera. Philitis is excited, his aura is exploding with crimson pulsations but he manages to contain himself in the interests of science.

"Can you tell me a little about how you did that?"

"I did it with time," I tell him as I open the tuna. "Time is a substance, but I've already explained this." I find Philitis' contained over-excitement disturbing.

"You better do something about your stomach Philitis or you're going to get sick."

"What do you mean?"

"You have an energy break there. When you get this excited you start losing an enormous amount of energy there."

"What should I do?"

"See a doctor. I'm not licensed to practice medicine."

"Would you like to go into the office Dr. Ccrab?" *I'm ready to puke.*

Philitis is right. The stench settling in the lab is impossible. As soon as Leo is finished eating we move into the Psychology office. The secretary immediately starts fanning her nose with a mimeographed sheet.

"I think your cat needs a bath Dr. Ccrab."

She knows it's not the cat of course but I'm too depleted to engage in repartee. I'm really out of it, half into another world, not quite back into this one. I take a pill for my stomach. I've been forcing my energy too much. These demonstrations. And too many readings. Inflation, I need the money. The secretary's aura reminds me of the mustard on yesterday's hotdog and she smells like old face powder.

"Are you tired?" asks Philitis.

"Moon opposition Mars square Neptune, Philitis. A little off balance."

"We can leave in a second. Can I use the phone Miss Haf-baker?"

"Acting Assistant Professors are not supposed to use the phone here. But go ahead."

"I have a confession," I blurt. "It was all fake."

"What was all fake?" Philitis is alarmed.

"The so-called experiment. Telepathy. Telepathy is fake. I'm

a fake. This office is fake. You Philitis, Miss Hafbaker, everything around us, all fake."

"I beg your pardon," says Miss Hafbaker.

"You don't have telepathic power?" asks Philitis.

"Yes I have telepathic power. But it's fake."

"I saw it with my own eyes Dr. Ccrab."

"What you see with your own eyes is fake."

"Sometimes I don't understand you."

"Understatement of the year. Did you ever read *The Tempest*, Philitis?"

"What's that?"

" 'These topless towers, / These vast, insubstantial pageants
rare, / All false, all clouds, / Players on a stage, which soon will
be but bare.' A play by Shakespeare. It's about a sorcerer." I
misquote intentionally, it's bad luck to use someone else's spells.

"No, I can't say I've read it. I'm a social scientist. But don't
worry, we have the whole experiment on videotape."

I take a fortune cookie out of my pocket, a freebie from Wang,
and toss it to Philitis. Trying to fend it off he catches it involun-
tarily and absently breaks it open.

"What does it say?"

Philitis reads: "Wealth and advancement are yours for the
faking."

"You see," I tell him. "Coincidence is no coincidence. It was
supposed to be 'taking' but Wang never proofreads."

Philitis makes his phone call. Leo comes over and looks up
into my eyes. Leo's coat is enormously furry, all black with white
chest and feet. Well, did you have enough tuna my friend, I
think.

"Snork snork," replies Leo, arching his back and rubbing his
cheek against my shoe. Though very conscious of his superiority

Leo is polite and appreciative, except when aroused by a female. Then forget it, he'll violate anything violable to get at the irresistible pussy. He then becomes impossible to control, as Leos do. I come very close to being a Leo. If my mother had waited a few more days . . .

"Is Professor Philitis here?" Like the sound of crystal or a bell I hear her voice with my whole body. I don't even turn around. Yet. Cathy Jane. Joan. June. Philitis, coming back from the phone, asks me if anything is wrong.

"Don't tell me. Blond. Face like Botticelli's Primavera. Comes from Santa Ana. Scorpio. Fish. Eyes blue as time. Doomed to be famous. About to have a love affair." With a fat, foul smelling middle-aged man. I turn around.

"Cathy June Grunion," announces Philitis. "This is Dr. Ccrab, Miss Grunion, the famous fortune teller."

Her eyes are blue and blank like a cartoon. Her aura, a beautiful pearl grey a little like Leo's, flares pink at the edges. I wish I had shaved this morning. Or even yesterday morning.

"The Dr. Boris O. Ccrab who writes the astrology column?" asks Cathy June in a little girl voice. I'm already in love. I already know it's going to make me unhappy. Fish. Grunion. Pig. Clover Bottom who was brought in as a look-alike when the original actress was hospitalized for "exhaustion" is the movie's main attraction. It is claimed that Miss Bottom was discovered by a well known fortune teller of Drackenstein's acquaintance who predicted stardom for her.

"You've read it?" Everything now depends on being cool. Control. Absence of passion. Yet it goes against the grain. But if I want to succeed I'll have to refrain. I've got to sell Cathy June to Drackenstein so as Clover Bottom she can get back what's mine.

"Really," says Cathy June. "Wow. This is really lucky."

"Luck is not merely luck Cathy June," I tell her. She's wearing one of those backless little dresses girls usually wear to cover their bikinis, in this case not covering one. Philitis is staring so hard it's embarrassing, though she doesn't seem to mind. What does she think of me I wonder and simultaneously realize I can't read her mind. I'm so surprised I actually stagger, my mouth falling open, as if in the act of leaning on something that unaccountably is no longer there. To cover myself I scoop up Leo and put him on my shoulder.

"I gave you an A on the paper, Cathy June," says Philitis. "It was really good." *Actually it deserved a C.* He hasn't screwed her but he's trying hard.

"An A," says Cathy June. "Neat-o. I thought I blew it."

"And you're an actress, Cathy June," I tell her.

"Really. How did you guess Dr. Ccrab?"

"Boris. I didn't guess."

"Are you really a psychic?"

"Ask Philitis here."

"Dr. Ccrab is as real as they come. In fact I'll be talking about him in the course." By this time Philitis is thoroughly inflamed. His aura is a throbbing purple flare and he smells like a raunchy tom cat. Cathy June's aura also shows excitement. She secretes an odor similar to Martel's V.S.O.P. I think of my own characteristic scent, desperately wonder why I can't read her mind. Is it because love is blind? Deprived of my main weapon I feel my potency ebbing away. Old. Fat.

"Thanks for the compliment Philitis. Maybe I can arrange a special demonstration for Cathy June."

"Did you want to make an appointment for that conference Cathy June," asks Philitis, pointedly ignoring me. "I'm free this

evening." *What's this crackpot trying to pull?* Leo. Look closely.
Green and brown. Svengali.

"What do you mean crackpot," I tell Philitis.

"I didn't say that," objects Philitis.

"Keep your insults to yourself. I'm a sensitive man, that's why
I can read your mind."

"Can you read everyone's mind?" asks Cathy June.

"Almost always."

"Okay, what am I thinking?"

"How can I read your mind when at the moment I can't even
read my own?"

"Gee. Try to guess."

"I told you I never guess."

"Really," says Cathy June laughing. "Maybe there's nothing to
read."

"I bet you're thinking of meeting me tonight," says Philitis.

"For sure," says Cathy June. She jiggles slightly in his direction. *I've got it made*, thinks Philitis. I'm about to slip over the
brink of a helpless depression. I lift Leo off my shoulder and
point him at her.

"Is that your pussy cat?" Cathy June skids into that tone
women reserve for babies and furry things. *Hey, wait a minute,
that's not fair*, thinks Philitis. I ignore him.

"Yes, this is Leo. I think Leo would like to make your acquaintance."

Cathy June dances over to me obviously very much taken with
Leo.

"Hey, wait a minute," says Philitis. But Cathy June is already
petting Leo in my arms.

"Oh, what a supernice pussy cat you are. What a furry puss.
Are you a boy or a girl?"

"Errow," obliges Leo.

"He's male. Unfixed. That's probably why he likes you so much."

Cathy June laughs. A bell again, crystal vibrations through my body. "Oh what a big, handsome, furry puss. What a lion. What a big, furry lion. I could kiss him."

"If you look into his eyes you'll notice one is green and one is brown. Like most Nepalese. Do you see?"

"Okay, no. They both look brown."

"You have to look closely, you have to look very closely."

"Oh wait a minute. Spacey. I think I'm beginning to see what you mean."

"You have to look carefully. It takes a while. His eyes change a lot depending on his mood. Just like mine. My eyes are brown and green, brownish green, brown or green, depending on my mood. When I'm aroused for example my eyes are green. I think they must be green right now, for example. Are my eyes green?"

"Yes, for sure. I see what you mean. Your eyes are green, Dr. Ccrab."

"Boris."

"Boris," repeats Cathy June.

"Why don't you come to my place for a reading Cathy June."

"That'd be real neat. Whenever. Golly."

"What about that conference?" asks Philitis. *You old Svengali.*

"What's wrong with tonight," I ask Cathy June.

"Nothing. Al*right*."

By this time Philitis is just standing there with his mouth open, his aura an angry crimson. I toss him a fortune cookie. The fortune says, "You are the master of almost every situation."

Hello this is Madame Lazonga I'm not here. Cards stars palm

reading crystal gazing. Luck is not merely luck. I did it with time. Dr. Roxoff called? Whether you know what's happening anymore is the question. It's all fake. A sorceress of sorts. Expresso digresso. Think sideways. I can read your mind Clara. Maybe there's nothing to read. Wang says you're splitting again. You have to look closely blank and blue. Roxoff says hallucinations. Svengali. Off the deep end. I dial Lazonga. The signal is interrupted by her voice.

"Hello this is Madame Lazonga I'm not here. Please leave your name and number on the tape and indicate whether you are interested in cards, stars, palm reading, crystal gazing or general consultation."

"This is Boris, Clara. I know you're there and you know what I'm calling about." I'm familiar with all of Lazonga's little tricks, this one was to filter out crank calls, like from me.

"Dr. Roxoff called?"

"He didn't have to call, I know what's happening anyway."

"Whether you know what's happening anymore is the question, C.c."

"Roxoff is my client."

"You can have him. I'm not trying to steal him."

"I can read your mind Clara, even over the phone. You've been talking to Wang."

"Wang says you're splitting again, you're hearing the voices?"

"Yes. Right now I'm hearing yours."

"Roxoff says hallucination. Schizophrenia. We don't want you off the deep end again. Last time we thought you weren't coming back."

"Roxoff would do better to worry about his Moon-Uranus conjunction. I'm going through some changes and the deep end is where change happens, where everything gets fluid and strange."

"C.c. I don't deny the occult exists but it's trivial in face of the facts. And fact is our fate. Remember we're professionals. We shouldn't take ourselves too seriously."

"Your problem is you've never been able to decide whether you're a fortune teller or a bank teller." Lazonga works in a bank. "Since I don't even believe in selves there's not much chance I'm going to take any of them very seriously. One thing I do take seriously is unprofessional conduct, including interference with someone else's practice, okay?" I hang up. Leo jumps onto my lap.

Cards stars palm reading. Planet of beauty. Hallucinations. Schizophrenia. Venus in Scorpio. As the end approaches the goal recedes. The deep end is where. All I have to do is keep my cool. Including the power to destroy yourself. The occult exists fluid and strange. The emotions of others. Expresso digresso. It will be dusk. I'm moving around my parlor watering my herbs and exotic plants, opening a can for Leo. I am directing my powers to Drackenstein's repentance. Cathy June will be like my daughter to his son, and through them we'll have a little fun. As Clover Bottom she'll realize her ambition, while Drackenstein will fall into perdition. In all this Cathy June is just my tool. All I have to do is keep my cool. And yet I know the truth at the beginning, that as the end approaches the goal recedes. But Cathy June is about to knock. I settle myself quickly at the table behind my crystal ball.

"Come in," I say.

There's a knock at the door.

"I said come in."

Cathy June enters. "Hi Boris, did you see me coming?"

"Sit down. Look at me." I look into her blue-as-time eyes. The room is dim. Her expression is calm, trusting as I trace her chart. I sense that she gives herself up easily, gladly to any kind of authority figure. Herself charismatic, she is very responsive to charisma, an excellent subject for hypnosis. I don't tell her that. What I tell her is to lie down on the couch.

"Venus in Scorpio. The planet of beauty rises in the sign of sensual power in trine to Neptune, the planet of glamour on the cusp and ruling the house of career. Born in Scorpio, you have the power to create and destroy, including the power to destroy yourself. While not very emotional, you are extremely vulnerable to the emotions of others which you cannot withstand and which threaten to sweep you away. Scorpio is a fixed water sign. Ice. Threatened by heat."

"Really," Cathy June murmurs.

"On the other hand this makes you a good performer, very responsive to the needs of an audience. Reinforced by strong Leo. Mars in Pisces emphasizes sensuality and receptivity."

I'm sitting close behind her in a chair as she reclines on the couch. She's wearing a t-shirt through which her nipples nose and a short skirt that flatters her tanned legs.

"You take a certain pleasure in the voluptuousness of surrender."

She nods. "For sure." Her eyes are diffuse, glazed.

"You are susceptible to willpower and tend to lose your self in the other. Moon in Libra. Cultivate firmness and consistency. Mars rules the mid-heaven and your ambition will help you."

She sighs, nods.

"You had a difficult, a very difficult childhood. Saturn intercepted in fourth, Fortuna square Pluto in Cancer. Also Mars in

Pisces quincunx Neptune, you have difficult relations with men.
Not to mention Venus semisextile Uranus from an uncongenial
sign."

"Truly, you're so right."

"Moon square afflicted Saturn. You probably won't have children. I'm sorry."

"I've never really wanted any."

"It may cheer you to know you'll make a lot of money. Jupiter
on eighth cusp. Moon in fourth indicates insecurity, need for
final peace, evasion of reality. The distribution of planets shows
a concern for externals. Also a severe conflict between regeneration and degradation, destruction and transcendence. The way
out is found in the eighth house through increased feeling and
sensitivity. This is also the house of death. Death will be peaceful. Avoid drugs."

"I never use drugs. Even marijuana. They space me out."

"Then you don't have to worry."

"Can I ask questions?"

"Of course."

"Okay, will I be famous?"

"Yes."

"When?"

"I can fill you in with a palm reading."

"Whatever."

I sit next to her on the couch and take her hand, opening it in
mine.

"Smooth fingers. Impulsive. Girdle of Venus sweeping toward Mount of Moon, very unusual, indicating strong erotic
responsiveness. The Line of Fate indicates love. The Line of
Heart indicates love."

"Can you tell what I'm thinking?"

"I told you no. But your aura just changed from powder blue fringed with pink to a kind of throbbing rose. I can also read lips."

"Truly. I'm into it," she says in her little girl voice.

I lift Cathy June toward me and kiss her. I can also read bodies. I watch my hand moving under her clothes like an animal. Her breath deepens, she remains still. I lift her t-shirt, Gauguin tits. Corpomancy. I'm really into it. Clover Bottom instant notoriety. Supposedly dead turned up today. Couldn't wait. Can I come look-alike exhaustion.

> deer Bore,
>     im really into it. couldn't wait 4 u 2 call so came over.! its 2 much, im just 22 hi. your some kind of stud.! excuse my spelling be sides i dont need 2 spell you got me under yours 4 sure. i am so strung out on you. i am really just 2 superspacey. PS u wurent here so i left this under the door.!
>                                                        LUV, Cathy June

"The first thing I notice about the handwriting is the height of the strokes, which indicates a tendency to exhibitionism. The lack of space between the letters suggests fear of being alone. The voluptuous loops and curves imply a heightened sexuality, while the diminished i's indicate underdeveloped ego. The irregular flow of the script and its erratic slant are signs of an unstable personality in need of constant gratification. This is a constellation often found in persons with inclinations to alcoholism, vice, drugs or other addictions. The carefulness of the f's, t's, l's, and d's show a certain calculation as well as an almost touching need for admiration and attention. The total conventionality of the lettering, combined with its maladroitness, indicates a lack of taste and originality. I find this an ominous and

doom laden script, Boris," says Lazonga, handing back the note.
"If I were you I'd leave this girl alone."

"I wasn't asking for advice, Clara, just an analysis."

"Then you already know what you should do," says Lazonga.
"She's not worth it."

"I know what I'm going to do. She's not worth it but she will
be worth it. Are you sure you're not jealous?"

"Your problem as a psychic has always been your lack of
insight into women."

"If you took the bandana off your head and stopped hiding
behind the gypsy number you'd be easier to understand." Lazonga, a striking woman in her thirties with strong nose and
black hair, is addicted to veils and mystifications.

"You love the obvious but I'm a chameleon, so for me disguise
is self-revelation," says Lazonga.

"If the end of our affair was make-believe you sure fooled
me."

"That's always been my tragedy."

What will happen is vampires what will happen is you have
no idea what's happening. Shooting out of sequence it's out of
order. Expresso digresso. Producer-director Rod Drackenstein's
shoestring production. Topless bottom wreaks havoc. About to
meet a fat aging fortune teller eating farrow. Taking too many
pills as the camera waits. Bring me back a ham sandwich. What
will happen is sitting in Nate'n Al's in Beverly Hills, Rod
Drackenstein and Victor Plotz, eating their breakfast lox and
bagels, Plotz looking like someone's fat uncle Drackenstein in
his off-white suit and open collared pink shirt like a tennis
champ. Plotz wipes a smudge of cream cheese off his lip with a
napkin and looks up.

"Something about this place makes me eat like a pig," says
Plotz. "Do you realize Mia Farrow's name means 'my little pig'?

Names are important, mine used to be Plotzick. Think about it. Hollywood is a sow that eats its farrow."

"That would make a great film," says Drackenstein.

"What, sows eating farrow?"

"No. 'My little pig.' As a title," says Drackenstein.

"Hey, you got something there. It opens vistas. As a sex film."

"Maybe we could put it in the vampire series," says Drackenstein. "Let's see, what do we have so far. *I Was a Teenage Vampire, Vampires on Wheels, Surfboard Vampire, Vampire From Outer Space*, what ever happened to the executive vampire concept where the vampire takes over a corporation?"

"That was when we were working with Miracle. He said no political allegory. Besides we need something fresh, we've bled vampires white already. Something fresh. 'My little pig,' what does that suggest? The little girl next door, your neighbor's daughter with hotpants, a hint of incest."

"Disgusting, Victor. Ugly. Grotesque. I think we got something here. Work it up. Give me a short treatment. I can see it now, a soft porn gem. It will all depend on a sexy new face. I think it might fly."

Producer-director Rod Drackenstein's shoestring production, *My Little Pig*, has grossed an amazing eight million dollars in eight weeks and attendance is mounting. The success of *Pig* has given its young star, Clover Bottom, instant notoriety, if not fame, in her first film. Miss Bottom, who was brought in as a look-alike when the original actress was hospitalized for "exhaustion," is the movie's main attraction. What will happen is in another part of the story off in the distances, Drackenstein is cruising in his sloop out of Newport Beach sailing with his son, hoping for reconciliation, I can feel the Santa Ana start to blow, howling hot and dry in my head, whipping up the waves and forcing the sloop out to sea. No hope of getting back to shore,

they head for Catalina and dock at Avalon. Sometimes you have
to sail the wrong way to catch the right wind. Think sideways.
By coincidence the same winds prevent O. U. Miracle's sea plane
from coming in at San Pedro, and, short of fuel, he heads back to
Catalina. That evening, they find themselves in the same restaurant with a wide angle view of Avalon Bay and share a table at
dinner. This is not the beginning of their relation. The beginning is way back in the sixties where they are brothers in the
fraternity of the New Left, followed by a friendship outlasting
the failure of the Movement into the seventies when, despair
taking the form of greed, they have a bitter business dispute.
Now because of the circumstances, they're reminded of *The
Tempest*, or Drackenstein is, Miracle never having read it, and
Drackenstein talks about the play's spirit of reconciliation. And
the possibility of his working with Universal-International
again. Miracle smells reconciliation in the air, both of them
surviving narrow escapes, out here together by chance in isolated idyllic Avalon, away from the greed and ambition of the
world, face to face. He smells reconciliation in the air and
decides to play it for what it's worth.

"You have," he says, "Clover Bottom's contract sewn up. Call
me at U.Ip whenever you're ready. We'll take a meeting."

"What exactly does that mean?"

Miracle gestures with the palm of his hand. "Trust me," he
says. "We'll make a deal."

Meanwhile back in the foreground, I'll be consolidating my
relation with Cathy June. "I'm in love," I announce to Dong
Wang. Wang is in his place. His place is the third stool from the
left at the bar of The Fat Black Pussy Cat. My place is the fourth
stool from the left. If we walk into The Fat Black Pussy Cat and
we find people in our places we don't find other places, we don't
say anything, we simply beam very heavy psychic vibrations at

the victims. It always works. Fast. Especially if both of us concentrate simultaneously on one of these unfortunates. Some leave quietly as if suddenly remembering an important appointment, others start scratching and fidgeting and finally go to the other end of the bar, some have sneezing fits and move to a booth complaining of a draft. Those who insist on hanging around awhile might for example slowly turn green and end up making panic dashes toward the rest room. Simple minded stuff I admit, but it's unlucky to let anyone take your place. Today the bar is empty as I sit down next to Dong Wang.

"Listen," says Wang, "one day you tell me you're going to die the next you tell me you're in love. Love and death. These symptoms have happened with you before Boris."

"It's happened before and it will happen again. Like clouds that pass and are replaced by other clouds that pass."

"Your recent melancholy is a bore. My Master knew how to make people bounce. He could make people bounce from up to a distance of ten feet away, a move called Making the Sparrow Hop, very rare. When challenged to a fight he would just sit there and make his opponent bounce. Amusing to watch someone hopping up and down like a rubber ball for no apparent reason. He would sometimes do it to back-sliding students. I would like to make you bounce."

"I had an illumination," I say. "A blinding light beyond which. Ego death."

"You mean death of this avatar," says Wang. "Who says you have to die to be reincarnated. It's probably that young girl you've been fucking. A little reincarnation like that never hurt anyone, especially you. How do you get these women to fall for you anyway?"

"I hypnotize them."

"You prick."

"I know. What can I do?"

"Could you hypnotize one for me?"

"I thought you have a powerful love potion."

"Yeah," says Wang. "One drop mild letch, two drop pure horniness, three drop grand passion. But it has unpredictable side effects."

"What about four drop?"

"It's a beautiful death. It was a mistake to hypnotize this young girl Boris. Be careful with her. Don't get in over your head."

"Don't worry," I assure him. "In a little while she'll be completely under my control."

"Or you under hers. One thing about your predictions about yourself Boris. They're always wrong."

"They're not wrong. They have a statistical probability. If they don't happen to me they'll happen to someone else. If they don't happen this way they'll happen that. I need, we all need, a certain plausibility in our lives. Beyond which nothing. Astrology is a flat system. Like life, it doesn't refer to anything beyond itself. That's why it works."

"And when it doesn't work?" asks Wang.

"That's when it gets interesting, improbable, where things get fluid and strange. People think the business of a fortune teller is to know the future. On the contrary, it's to define the known in order to discover the unknown, to predict the unpredictable."

Meanwhile far away at a gathering of the stars, Clover Bottom is doing her strange trick with the crowd, presenting herself on stage like the sacrificial virgin, passive focus of a mass identity, delicious, edible, the crowd roars. Here, now, she's still a kid, despite the go-go dancing, the Vegas experience and the rest, walking down Rodeo with her, watching the Rolls roll by, the Mercedes the shiny Porsches in the middle of Beverly Hills, all of it an advertisement for itself. I'm feeling the pleasure of walking around in it all not wanting anything while she can barely restrain her wide-eyed envy. I cater to her fascination in Nate 'n Al's.

"Over there, that's Rory Calhoun," I tell her.

"You got to be kidding," says Cathy June, "right over there?"

"And that's Roger Corman just walking out."

"Really. How do you know that's really Rory Calhoun?"

"Who knows? Maybe it's somebody doing an impression. You want the real thing?"

"I don't know," says Cathy June. "What is it?"

"Power. Everybody has it."

"Really. What kind of power?"

"A kind of power that when I was a kid I used to be frightened and ashamed of but that was irresistible, that I tried desperately to avoid suppress and destroy but gave into again and again and then began, to my horror, to admit into my consciousness, that I struggled with only to discover that the struggle itself was a kind of giving in. From that time on I became stupid, almost mute, got bad marks in school—I, who had always been the smartest kid in the class—but I had a secret knowledge that was potent but that I had no idea how to deal with, the power of my by then explosive feelings, and the little magic wand of my sex which I had only to wave and the world would be transformed, naturally sex got dragged into the general confusion. In fact I think I was a little crazy, maybe all teenagers are crazy but incredibly unhappy, isolated, strange. Then the seizures began."

"What seizures?"

"Shaking, babbling, cramps. During which I was forced to confront all those things I didn't want to know, wanted to keep out of my mind. But during those seizures I was out of my mind, and brought all those things back into it. At first I'd just have the feeling I knew what someone was thinking. When I began to realize I was always right I was terrified. I really didn't want to know what people were thinking, especially about me. I once accidentally read the mind of a blind date and felt really humiliated. You have to be careful, sometimes you eavesdrop on really embarrassing things. And some minds are really perverted, violent, impoverished. Then there were my hunches, hunches that always turned out to be right. For years I pigeonholed all this stuff into the category of 'just feelings, everybody has them.' Until I finally got the idea that either I was going to admit to my 'feelings' or they were going to destroy me. I began to recognize that my feelings were my power."

"Really. I couldn't deal with that."

"To you it's scary because you're afraid of feeling. And so was I. I love order. Feeling is disruptive, disorderly. But it's the whole trip. It makes you happy and it makes you unhappy. It makes you conscious or it makes you numb. It makes you smart or it makes you dumb."

"Is it true you used to do readings for all those Hollywood people?"

"I've done some of the biggies. Eddie, Jack, Rita, Frank."

"Well if you have so much power how come you don't put me in touch with some of your Hollywood connections?"

"When the stars are right. Be patient Cathy June. Sometimes I think you only love me for my power."

"You old turkey."

"So you think I'm old?"

"Older men turn me on. They have all the power."

At the same place but a different time I see Drackenstein and

Plotz eating their breakfast lox and bagels watching the entities and nonentities. "Hey there's Buddie over there."

"He's been fading, huh?" comments Plotz.

"Fading? He's been invisible for years. Of course I haven't been exactly front page myself since Miracle finessed me out of United-International. But I've been keeping a certain notorious visibility with the exploitation crap. Now since *My Little Pig*'s taken off Miracle's got his eye on Clover Bottom's box and I've got Clover Bottom. We had an interesting encounter out on Catalina."

"You got total control?"

"Total. So keep Clover's talent in mind, you know, keep it simple. Tits and ass with a lot of general admission culture and morality. It could be an interesting property. I sent Miracle the treatment." Drackenstein flips through the pages. "Try to get hold of Los Angeles in the final version. Shaky City, as the CB people call it."

"What do I know about it Rod? I'll never get used to Los Angeles. I'm a Brooklyn boy."

"You've only been here twenty years Victor. Life in the patios. The way people talk. Zipping around the freeways. The tall dusty palms, the way they rattle in the wind. That's not in there but you can put it in. That's what I want, the feel of the city. I mostly grew up here you know. Little things you remember. Learning to drive on the Santa Anita parking lot vast and empty in the evening. A far view of the oil rigs on Signal Hill from a second floor window near Wilshire and Western. Actually seeing the train going down Santa Monica Boulevard ghostly after midnight. A girl like our heroine grows out of this city like the exotic flora in the tacky parks, fuchsia, bougainvillea, bird-of-paradise, just like Cathy June Grunion. I can see her in the seediness of MacArthur Park. Or hanging out with the last

hippies in Venice. Or a kid bopping past the weirdos on Hollywood Boulevard head full of neon. There are a thousand Cathy
Junes in this city, including Clover Bottom. All doomed. Dumb.
No depth, no culture, no resources. Born to be exploited. But
beautiful in their small, touching way, the intensity of their
hope, their wasted desire, their cheap hooker innocence. That's
the story I want Victor. It's not only Los Angeles it's America.
Nathanael West was right on, the fury of their disappointment
leads straight to the flames, to violence, to mass murder."

"Met a guy the other day," says Plotz, "I ask him where'd you
get the Mercedes, he says it comes from investing money he
won in a Corona pool. I say you mean del Mar, he says, no, Juan.
This fucking monkey won ten thousand smackers in a pool on
how many Corona bodies they'd dig up. How do you like that.
Sickorama. Hey, here comes cutey pie. She's got a face like a
bellybutton. Look at the heads turn."

Clover is wearing a version of one of those little things girls
wear to cover their bikinis, without a bikini, giving her a kind of
super blond beach bunny look.

"Sit down," says Drackenstein. "You look sixteen this morning. What'll you have?"

"A coke. I feel sixty-five. It's too early."

"A coke at ten in the morning," says Plotz. "You got a habit
already. Hi sweetie. How'd you like my script?"

"It's me. I hate it," she laughs.

"You see my vision Victor," continues Drackenstein. "This
girl is on the edge of failure, back to Vegas, dope, occasional
tricks, when her father's astrological studies tell him she's got it,
it's in the stars, and he starts pushing her career but she can't
handle the scene. He thinks he's doing her a favor but it's like
Greek tragedy, the very thing that saves her kills her, it's all
there from the very start. Only it's got to move, it's got to be

simple, and I've got to typecast the parts, like the producer is a heavy, the scene is really evil, and his daughter is a dummy. Something that films easy and fast."

"And cheap," says Plotz.

"And cheap," says Drackenstein. "We have a low budget but don't worry about it. Let the camera create the subtleties. An audience doesn't need a whole feminist dialectic when it's looking at a sad beautiful face."

"Or ass," says Plotz.

"Cool it Victor. Remember you're writing a story about liberation. *The Tempest* is paternalistic. With these new characters everything changes. Hands off Mandy! Free Cal! Propper improper! And Los Angeles is part of it. The beaches, the wild houses, the crazy restaurants."

"L.A. restaurants," says Plotz. "I go into this fancy French restaurant on La Cienega the other day and ask the waitress what's this veal mornay a la poopick oo la la, and she says, oh that's just the way it's cooked. I know a hip health food restaurant in Beverly Hills that's got so many plants in it a friend of mine got lost on the way to the men's room and had to piss behind a potted figtree. They had to call out the Forest Search and Rescue Team. He says he met Smokey the Bear while he was in there and asked him about his contract. I know another restaurant around here that's so bad they got a sign on the door that says, Sorry, We're Open."

Drackenstein looks at his watch. "All right let's wrap it Victor, we have a tennis date. Clover's taking lessons. Want to come?"

"Nah, I feel good today," says Plotz, "why should I spoil it by doing something healthy. By the way, did you two see the bit in the *Times*?"

"Really. Let's see," says Clover.

### LITTLE PIG, BIG BOX

*Hollywood.* Producer-director Rod Drackenstein's shoestring production, *My Little Pig*, has grossed an amazing eight million dollars in eight weeks, and attendance is mounting. The success of *Pig* has given its young star, Clover Bottom, instant notoriety, if not fame, in her first film.

Miss Bottom, who was brought in as a look-alike when the original actress was hospitalized for "exhaustion," is the movie's main attraction. Reviewers have almost totally ignored the film as a whole and have focused attention on parts of Bottom's body, which is frequently seen nude. Critics have quibbled between her bust and bottom in trying to pin down her allure. Some reviewers are in neither camp and attribute her erotic appeal to that mysterious something that all movie goddesses have had. "Monroe had it, Bardot had it, and Bottom has it," one recently wrote.

Part of *Pig*'s success may be due to the mythology that surrounded it from the first. Said to reflect Bottom's life, this is denied by those involved with the film almost as frequently as they bring it up. Furthermore it is claimed that Miss Bottom was discovered by a well known fortune teller of Drackenstein's acquaintance, who predicted stardom for her. Whether Miss Bottom was a teenage prostitute who liked to invite gang sex, as in the film, is something she will not comment on. Drackenstein, however, has said that wild sexual adventures at an early age are not as unusual as they used to be for today's precocious young people. When asked why he makes frequent use of cinema vérité, he answers, "It's cheaper."

Drackenstein, who has turned out a score of films in recent years which hover between exploitation and porn, has said that his cinematic theory consists of three principles: "Make them fast, make them cheap, and make them pay." Some cinema buffs, who may take Drackenstein more seriously than he takes himself, claim that he has returned movie making to its early days, when the necessity for improvisation in order to reduce cost increased originality. Drackenstein has reportedly commissioned a new script for Bottom, based on Shakespeare's *Tempest*, a play about a fortune teller who is ambitious about his daughter's career.

Really. Cigar tubes monkey bars. I get off on coke. Hail Rosecranz Artesia Believed. Yellow grey. The sky changes from grey to yellow grey. The yellow Stingray cruising down the freeway. El Segundo Blvd. Rosecranz Ave. Redondo Beach Blvd. Artesia Blvd. Crenshaw Blvd. Down down the San Diego Freeway pinstripe weather striations in graphite-grey roadway under big jets coming in at Inglewoods past cigar tubes monkeybars candle flames of oil refineries to Laguna in her yellow Stingray the license plate says REALLY. Yellow dress yellow hair. The sky changes from grey to yellow grey to sunny blue down past Long Beach. I ask her if she gets off on accepting gifts from men she sleeps with.

"Really," says Cathy June.

"I mean the car. Don't drive so fast."

"I'm only going fifty. You know about that."

"I know about everything."

"I can see where going out with a psychic has its hangups."

"That's why you're always busy Thursday evenings." Cathy June is driving with one hand, sipping a can of coke with the other.

"I can't get into this trip."

"Suppose you stopped."

"Either he repossesses me or he repossesses the car don't

hassle me. I'm not really into him. Is that why you're so up-tight?" She drops her coke can out the window.

"You can get a big ticket for that one."

"I really get off on coke."

"Slow down please."

"I'm going forty-five. Boris? Is that why you're uptight?" asks Cathy June. "No answer?" says Cathy June.

"I wish I could read your mind," I say.

"Then I'd be like everyone else wait a minute. I can read yours. You're jealous. That's just super." She reaches over and pats my crotch. "Bore is jealous. The Big Bore is jealous. You turkey. I love your silvery hair. Your cat glow eyes. Okay you know you can make me stop if you want to. You got a spell on me. Only what am I gonna do for a car?" She shoves a cassette in the deck mouth and the car floods with soul thudding rhythms.

"Would you mind turning that off," I shout. She turns it off.

"What's wrong with Bob Dylan?"

"He's a Woody Guthrie ripoff."

"Who's Woody Guthrie?" She shoves another cassette in.

"How about this?"

"No," I shout. She turns it off. "What's wrong with Tom Waits?"

"He's a Louis Armstrong ripoff."

"No he's not. He's a Lou Reed, Jim Morrison ripoff." She puts on some Jim Morrison, something about cars hissing by the window, Hollywood bungalows, L.A. women, city of night city of light, I ask her to turn it off. She turns it off.

"Okay, what's wrong with Jim Morrison?"

"He's a nihilist."

"What's a nihilist?" she asks.

"No wonder I can't read your mind, there's nothing in it."

"That's what they're always telling me," she says. "But I think they're just too busy looking at the bod to notice."

"Spare me the baby talk," I tell her. "Otherwise I might send you dodo without din-din."

At a similar place in the network, at a time further off in the future, Rod Drackenstein and Clover Bottom are driving down the Golden State Freeway, where the overpasses crumbled in the quake, toward Newhall in Drackenstein's yellow Stingray, listening to a phone-in show on the radio whose subject is "do you live out your fantasies?" Drackenstein is wondering whether if you live them out they're really fantasies. I mean, he thinks, doesn't living out your fantasies show a certain lack of imagination? He feels he no longer has any fantasies, and he wonders whether it's because he's living them all out, or because, having dealt in fantasy so long as a director, he can no longer tell fantasy from reality. Clover isn't thinking about anything. She's flipping through Plotz's long treatment silently mouthing some of Mandy's lines like a child reading a comic book to itself.

"Gee, I don't know, Rod," she says finally. "This script. It means I have to act."

"Don't worry," answers Drackenstein, "just play yourself. Like last time."

"Really. That's too confusing."

"Leave it to me. I'm the director. Wait a minute, I want to hear this. Let's see if Barb from Downey lives out her fantasies." He turns up the radio:

I mean (says Barb on the radio) I hope you're not going to think this is vulgar or something Bill.

Why of course not dear. The thought never even entered

my head. In fact on this show the concept of vulgarity doesn't even exist, I wouldn't even know what it means, so you just go ahead and don't let it bother your little poopick.

Really. Okay. I have this fantasy? And I got it from this movie?

Which movie, dear?

Okay, this movie with Clover Bottom? Where she ties up this dude?

"Hey, you hear that?" says Drackenstein.

And she forces him to make love to her. Right.

For sure. And he really likes it? Okay, well I did it with my boyfriend? He's a Capricorn?

You actually tied him up?

Really.

"Really," says Clover.

What did you tie him up with?

With handcuffs?

With handcuffs. Where'd you get handcuffs?

At the store?

And then what happened?

Okay, well he really dug it?

And how did you like it?

Al*right*. It was just super.

"Al*right*," says Clover.

So, is that it?

No.

What else?

Okay, well I lost the keys?

You lost the keys to the handcuffs?

Really. Okay, and while I was looking for them Linda came in?

And who may I ask is Linda?

Okay, she's my sister? She's seventeen, okay?

Yes, go on dear.

Okay, and she tried it too? With my boyfriend I mean?

Wasn't your boyfriend getting tired?

No. He's a Capricorn.

"Al*right*!" says Clover. "This dude's some kind of stud."

Anything else Barb?

Okay, and then I told my girlfriend Connie about it? She's this *really* neat chick. And she tried it with this stud, okay? Okay, and then they liked it so much we all bought a lot of handcuffs and a bunch of us did it at the party on Friday? And now the stores in Downey are all out of handcuffs?

Well. What can I tell you dear. Have you tried Bell-flower?

Really. Well Bill?

Yes dear.

Do you know if Clover Bottom is making any more movies soon?

Listen to that," says Drackenstein. "That's you. Clover Bottom. You're worth a million bucks. You're certainly living out your fantasies."

"Really," says Clover. "My fantasies are the only thing I have."

Meanwhile, back in another part of time to the south, Cathy June and I will be rolling through the chaparral hills of Laguna Freeway into town and the Pacific Coast Highway. I see us climbing down wooden steps to the beach on a steep cliff carpeted with ice plant, lavender and yellow flowers. She strips to bikini underwear her underwear is her bathing suit that's the chic thing. I pull my pants down over my sagging belly to my trunks and stretch myself next to her. Blue, Catalina Island on horizon, white sails, blue, a few mothers with young kids.

"I used to come here in my beach bunny days," Cathy June says. "I'm blissing out."

"Sun's in Scorpio," I tell her.

"Is that good or bad?"

"You'll have to make some big decisions. Rod Drackenstein is casting a new film."

"Rod Drackenstein isn't going to pick me out of cattle call."

"Jupiter is in Aries. A lot of power is on the loose. Seek union with superior consciousness but be careful. Always ask whether the circumference justifies the center. A lot is at stake."

"That's a heavy trip for a sunny day. Are you telling my fortune?"

"If you don't want to know I won't tell you. I don't tell anyone what they don't want to know, or even sometimes what they do. People should be able to read their own minds. When you start reading your own mind you'll be able to tell your own fortune."

"You're such a crab." She grins at me, running her hand through my thinning hair. "Come on, I want to show you something neat." She springs up and walks down the beach, I follow enjoying the cling of her peaches. Down at the end of the cove there's a rocky point. We wade out alongside it and there's a cave sloping up into the cliff, we splash in, up onto an underground beach in the green gloom, the water sloshing, roaring when a wave rolls in through the cave mouth. Sea crabs, bluish red, scuttle sideways across the floor, disappear into rock pools.

"See," says Cathy June, "this is where the crabs live."

"Well I feel right at home," I tell her. "Take your clothes off."

"Yes, master," she says in her little girl voice, but instead pulls down my trunks. "You see," she says, "hard and red, like a crab, but soft inside." She takes me in her mouth, I almost come right away, for a while it's nip and tongue I slide out just in time.

"Why am I so into you?" she says. "You make me just too superhigh. I don't understand it. Tell me you love me, you never said that to me."

"It's bad luck to say it. Some things you just have to come at sideways. Who was . . . Dick?"

"You mean Rick? What do you know about Rick?"

"You made love with him here. That's why you brought me here, it already has erotic power for you. Someone else's."

"No, really, I just spaced it out. Plus I lost it on the Golden State Freeway in the back of a van when I was fourteen okay? You can't be jealous of all the men I've made love with."

"You live on them."

"Okay, I dig getting gifts from lovers, okay? I get off on taking money for fucking someone it really turns me on."

"It really turns me off. Turn over." I pull her underwear off and set her on all fours, making love to her from behind, hard and mean, full of spite. I feel surrounded, and lost inside her as if in thought, a thought that comes without thinking, from some-where else, lost in the sudden confusion of being simultaneously

inside Cathy June Grunion and the sex goddess Clover Bottom.
Faster and faster, superhigh, silver cat glow, thinking red, water
sloshing, sea crabs scuttling, tide rising, withdrawing, cresting,
roaring, drowning, oblivious, drowning.

"Bore?" Hugging on the sand. "Think something quick. A
color. Don't say anything."

*Red.*

"You're thinking red. Bore, I can read your mind. Wait a
minute, this is too spacey. You're thinking about giving me a
gift, you're thinking about paying me. I can't handle it."

"Wait a minute wait a minute, you were thinking hard shell
soft inside . . ."

*. . . like a crab.*

*Should I give you a gift.*

*You're giving me everything I want. It makes me superhigh. I
don't get into it with other men. I am really into being your lady,
I am just too into you and all your trips. I love to know my
things make you pleased, be by you, make you more into me. I
dig it. I love to see you jealous. It doesn't hassle my scene. I love
to see you all into me. You make those spaces in me. It's too
crazy, it's just too spacey the way I relate with you. I'm so into
your fucking me. Your silver cat glow is so far out to see. I'm
completely into doing whatever you want . . .*

I'll sit up abruptly.

"Boris. What's wrong?"

"You're dreaming. You don't know what you want. Today you
think you love me tomorrow you'll be into some other fantasy."

Cathy June is suddenly on the edge of tears. "I've never seen
you in such a bad mood," she says. I stand up.

"Sorry. This is giving me a headache. Let it go. Let's get out of
here and take a walk."

You tend. Lazonga. You tend obsessive. Lazonga's voice starts sounding in my head. "You tend to have strong relations with women, as we know," I hear her saying. "Obsessive. Your Moon opposition Mars, Sun in Cancer. But also your Scorpionic energy comes into play plus Sun in eighth house conjunct Pluto, power of regeneration. Your need to transform things must be fulfilled to complete your identity and leave it behind. Even at the risk of destruction, or perhaps only at the cost of it, like the phoenix. You can realize your power only on behalf of others, but if it doesn't work for them it destroys them. Scorpio is either-or. Sun conjunct Pluto which rules the eighth house also means tremendous power but it's tricky. Plutonian energy driving toward invisibility, mystery of eighth house, also death and regeneration. Be careful. It might be best to leave her alone."

We're in Lazonga's green stucco bungalow out in Venice. I don't remember how I got there.

"I can't do that," I say.

"I know. Sun square Uranus. You can't listen to advice. Then take your fate in hand. Revise the plot."

"That means?"

"That means stop being obtuse and evasive, C.c. Cathy June is being destroyed in her Clover Bottom identity thanks to your success in promoting her to Drackenstein. The whole thing has to be reenvisioned. Use your power. We all make up our own scenarios, that's what it's all about."

"Nonsense, Clara. You've always given good readings and bad advice. Thanks all the same."

But on the way home I think about it and think maybe she's right, she probably is, and by the time I get to my house I've made up my mind to being less the scribe of destiny and try to take things more in hand.

Meanwhile, up in Drackenstein's office high in a building on Sunset and Doheny against the Hollywood Hills, Plotz and Drackenstein are having a conference about the script. On a clear day, when there is a clear day, you can see from Drackenstein's window across the bowl of Los Angeles out to the sometimes snowpeaked San Gabriel Mountains beyond Pasadena. Today it's hazy, the buildings downtown barely visible, the sky a color that is not blue not grey not brown not even white, that might best be described as blank. Drackenstein is trying to describe to Plotz his conception of the fortune teller.

"Have a heart, Rod," says Plotz. "I'm just a hack screenwriter. I don't know anything about fortune telling."

"This won't fly, Victor," says Drackenstein. "The concept is good but it's not convincing. You're going to have to run it through the typewriter again."

"What I hear you saying Rod is that you're not happy with my work," says Plotz.

"You hear correctly, Victor. And I want more tits in it. And ass. This is a vehicle for Clover Bottom, not Katherine Hepburn. Hey how did you get in here?"

"Astral projection," I say.

"Did we have an appointment?"

"Your secretary seemed to think so. I thought you needed technical advice."

"You know Professor Ccrab, don't you Victor. Victor's taking care of all the technical research." I catch Drackenstein's eye and hold it. *But as a matter of fact*, I think, *we could use some help*.

"But as a matter of fact," says Drackenstein, "we could use some help."

"Now wait a minute," says Plotz.

"No no, listen to me," says Drackenstein. "This thing needs

context. That's the hangup. We need the atmosphere, the ambience, the tone."

*I want this to be an authentic film,* I think, *no more of this exploitation crap.*

"I want this to be an authentic film," says Drackenstein. "No more of this exploitation crap. I don't need it anymore. I'm tired of being a running gag in the industry. Let's do something a little toney this time. You get the picture Victor?"

"Yes boss."

"Don't get wise. All right Professor, what's it like to be a fortune teller?"

"It's like there are mornings when you get out of bed," I tell him, "and you open up the dresser drawer and a voice says, 'Don't put on those sox! the green ones. Not today!' So you drop the malevolent green sox back in the drawer, tomorrow they'll probably be okay, and you put on some harmless red ones, that's what it's like to be a fortune teller. To listen to those voices that are always whispering in the back of your head. To listen to all of them, to listen carefully and to hear the ones most people can't hear because they don't listen. And to always believe them. Don't step on the cracks in the sidewalk. Don't wash your hands on Tuesday. Walk around the block before you get into your car. Enter the building through the left hand door not the right hand door. Don't answer the next two phone calls. These are the voices of your feelings. Sometimes they're voices and something they're feelings. Sometimes you don't know whether they're voices or whether they're feelings. Sometimes they're the same thing. For the fortune teller it doesn't make any difference, his feelings are voices, but for others, they need the voices, and that's what a fortune teller does, he gives voices to feelings."

"There you go, Victor," says Drackenstein. "The horse's

mouth. Run that through and see what comes out. All right, Professor, you're on. Tell me something. Can you predict when people are going to die?"

"Would you like me to predict when you're going to die?"

Drackenstein's aura goes pale and jumpy, rotting spinach smell of fear. "I'd rather you didn't."

"I didn't think so." Actually he's going to die of old age but let him worry.

Wang is sitting on his stool in the The Fat Black Pussy Cat when I walk in. "Where you been?" he says. "You look a little tired."

"I am. I just got back from an astral trip to the future."

"What about?"

"Business. Up at Drackenstein's office."

"Still hung up with that. How are things going with Cathy June?"

"I'm feeling guilty as hell lately," I tell him. "I'm afraid I'm selling her into some kind of prostitution."

"What do you think she was doing in Vegas?" says Wang.

"You think I should forget about Drackenstein."

"Yes."

"I can't," I say.

"I know. How long can you keep it up? You look like a ghost."

"I don't know. I'm really ambivalent. It's tiring doing three things at once. For example I'm also with Cathy June right now over at my place. Sometimes I feel a little schizoid. Fragmented."

"Sounds like you're getting overcommitted," says Wang.

"All of us are more than one person, Wang. The first person is a grammatical category, nothing more. Identity is a social phenomenon and faced with conflicting social needs, we crack.

Ccrab needs power and Ccrab needs love. I'm Ccrab but I is in quotes. I have to keep reminding myself who I am, that's how schitzy I'm getting."

"Are you really Ccrab?" asks Wang.

"Is this really happening?"

"I guess so."

"Then I guess I'm really Ccrab. I have to get back to my place now. Cathy June is upset." I get up and walk out the door. Wang goes to a pay phone at the end of the bar and dials my number.

"Hello," Cathy June answers, her voice panicky.

"Can I speak to Boris please?" asks Wang.

"Something's wrong with him," says Cathy June. "He's passed out. I'm freaking."

"Cathy June this is a friend of Boris'. It's a cataleptic fit. It sometimes happens to him."

"Cat of what?" Cathy June asks.

"It's like a trance. He'll come back soon. He should be coming back any minute."

"Wait a minute," says Cathy June after a pause. "Lie down."

"Hello Wang?" I say. "I'm back."

"Better watch that Ccrab. One day you won't be able to get back."

"So what," I tell him. "That's true of everybody."

Meanwhile, alone back at my bungalow, I'm soliloquizing to Leo on my lap. "I have a feeling, friend, that our plot is going fine. And when I have a feeling it's a little different from when other people have a feeling. Everything in order, Cathy June under control. I see it clear to Cathy June's assumption into the firmament in *My Little Pig*. I assume the guilt of power. My innocence is gone. I plot the order of fate from the planets of fortune. Unfortunately order always leads to doom, that's the secret meaning of tragedy."

"Errow," says Leo.

"You're bored. You're not interested in this kind of talk. Best not. I'll give you lunch. But wait, here comes Cathy June."

I get up and look out the window. Cathy June is pulling up to the curb in an old dented khaki beetle. She comes in with the news that she gave back the Stingray. "I had a strong feeling you were going to do that," I tell her.

"What's my reward?"

"You're going to get to ride around in another Stingray. But you have to do exactly what I tell you."

"I always do exactly what you tell me."

"You resent this?" I ask her.

"No. I thought you could read my mind now."

"Not today. It seems to be unpredictable. What are you doing?" Cathy June is lighting a cigarette with a matchbook.

"I'm lighting a cigarette," she says, lighting a cigarette. I snatch the matchbook.

"Are you mad?" I yell at her. "With a match from the back of the matchbook?"

"What's wrong?"

"That's very bad luck. Especially with Venus in Scorpio. You start from the left hand front of the matchbook and don't get out of order. I love you. Loose hair. Toe nails. Hot ice."

"Boris, what are you talking about?"

"Mars in Virgo. Fly glue. Sperm nuts."

"What does that mean?" asks Cathy June.

I double over. "I have no. Idea. Have to. Have. Sit."

She helps me to the couch where I lie down, shaking.

"Bore. What's wrong?"

"Cramps. Something like broken. Deep."

"Tell me what to do," says Cathy June.

"Cuh cuh can't stop. Truh truh trembling."

"Should I call the doctor?" She's wiping my forehead. My eyes turn back in my head.

"Nin nin no wuh . . ."

"Boris? I'm scared. Can you see me? I'm here. Cathy June."

The phone rings. She picks it up and hears Wang's voice saying, "Can I speak to Boris please."

"Something's wrong with him," says Cathy June. "He's passed out. I'm freaking."

"Cathy June this is a friend of Boris'. It's a cataleptic fit. It sometimes happens to him."

"Cat of what?" asks Cathy June.

"It's like a trance. He'll come back soon. He should be coming back any minute."

I get up off the sofa. I seem to feel all right. Very tired.

"Wait a minute," says Cathy June at the phone. "Lie down," she tells me. I take the phone from her.

"Hello, Wang?" I say. "I'm back."

"Better watch that Ccrab," says Wang. "One day you won't be able to get back."

"So what. That's true of everybody." We play our roles and leave the stage, never to return. The long black Rolls rolls down Wilshire driven by a chauffeur in a stetson singing romantic cowboy songs while I wait impatiently to arrive. Finally he pulls up in front of a park. "Can the cat see the cat seeing?" he says. I get out. There across a weed rimmed pool Cathy June stands waiting, while back at the car two men ask the cowboy for his autograph, then pull him out of the car still singing and put a

gun to his head. The cowboy holds some weird desperate note
from a cowboy song till it's cut off by a gunshot. I try to wade
across the pool to Cathy June but it's filled with a black oily
substance, bubbles rising heavily to the surface with a noise like
blup blup. Then she says, "Welcome to the pits." I wake up the
phone ringing it's her. She has a job at seven a.m. and she's
freaking out. She's afraid she won't make it.

"Jesus it's four a.m. You've got three hours."

"I've been up all night."

"Why?"

"Because I've been freaking out. I can't do it."

"All right. All right you want me to come over?"

"You couldn't."

"I could. I'm volunteering. All right?"

"Please."

The Plumyth gets me over to the Princess Gracia Apartments
on Fountain Avenue around five a.m. Cathy June is wrecked.
Her aura is ragged and pulsing in rapid twitches. She's sitting up
on her convertible bed wearing a thin shorty night gown in
some kind of stupor. I sit there next to her on the bed and put
my arms around her. "What's wrong?"

"I'm all strung out," she says tearfully. It suddenly comes to
me that she's been making love with someone. I draw back.

"All right who was it?"

"Who was what?"

"Who you were screwing a couple of hours ago."

"He wasn't anybody."

"Disgusting," I shout. "Pig."

"It's none of your stinking business," she shouts back.

I grab her by the shoulders and shake her. "Oink oink oink.
My little pig." She claws at my face and I throw her down on the

bed. We're screaming at one another, yowling like cats. I've got her pinned to the bed when the bitch grabs my balls so I can't move. We're locked on the bed together, immobile, neither of us giving up. But when my periscope rises I start to submerge and she knows she's going to win. She does. We make love furiously.

She's sleeping like an angel next to me when I get the distinct feeling that the man she was fucking earlier is the man who got her the bit she's worried about. I shake her shoulder.

"That bit in the film you're supposed to do this morning?"

She doesn't answer.

"You turned a trick last night for that job." She doesn't answer. Her eyes blink open. "I say you fucked this guy to get your bit."

"Okay, don't fuck with my career."

"Whoring around for penny ante bits? You call that a career?"

"Okay what am I gonna do?" Tears. "I've tried everything what am I gonna do get a job in the May Company? Go back to go-go dancing? What? What? What?" Her voice rising hysterically.

"Now listen to me." I put my hand on her chest it's heaving like hiccups. "What you're going to do is breathe. Take a deep breath. Breathe out slowly. In and then out. In one . . . two . . . three. Out three . . . two . . . one. In deeper. Out slower. That's it. That's better. Now you're calming down aren't you. Now you're much calmer. You are much calmer aren't you?"

"Much better. Much much better." She rolls her eyes at me. "Thanks Bore. Thanks for the artificial respiration."

"Now tell me about this job."

"Okay, it's called *Sargon*? Some kind of hairy epic? They're using that UniRoyal factory out on the Santa Ana that was built like some kind of Babylonian castle like where's Babylonia?"

"On the back lot. Now you're not going to make that job this morning okay Cath?"

"I'm not Bore?"

"Just keep breathing Cath. One . . . two . . . three . . . three . . . two . . . one."

"I guess not. Really. If you say so Bore." Breathing easy, closes her eyes. Then starts crying again.

"What now?"

"You mean I fucked that bastard for nothing?"

"Didn't you tell me you like sleeping with men you don't like?"

"Really. I can dig it."

"Why do you like to do that Cath?"

"Don't know Bore. Seems to give me some kind of rush."

"Did you ever think of going to a therapist Cath?"

"I been. Dr. Roxoff."

"Roxoff. You're kidding. He's one of my clients, an Aries. Worries about his Moon-Uranus conjunction. Was it effective?"

"Yeah, he wanted to fuck me."

"What did you want?"

"What I want is somebody to take care of me, okay? I've tried. I've worked hard. Once this producer, at least he said he was a producer, he called me up in the middle of the night? He said if I'd come over and perform an unnatural act for him and a few friends he'd give me a part? Okay, so I drive up from Hermosa Beach to Bel Air at 2 a.m., perform an unnatural act for a few hours, and end up on the way back with a flat tire on Sepulveda at six in the morning, the guy never got in touch. Things like that. I'm tired of it. I know it's not cool but I want somebody to tell me what to do. Tell me what to do and I'll do it."

"You make me very happy Cath."

"Me too. Now tell me what to do."

"What do you mean?"

"You said you were going to tell me what to do. So tell me. You're always telling me what not to do. So now tell me what to do."

"About what?"

"About everything. About my life. My career. Stay away from the casting couch. Plus no more penny ante extra jobs. Okay okay. So how do I make a living? I mean you got plenty of big studio connections with your clients, okay? Are you going to help me out a little or what?"

"No point worrying Cath. It all depends on coincidence. And coincidence is inevitable."

Stiff as a bullet Ccrab shoots straight up into the air. He rockets up so fast it feels like he's going slow spurts through the first layer of clouds with a soft plop the air gray then mustard then pink then blue and he's free soaring like a shark. Thunderheads look like distant cliffs an instant later like puffs of smoke like sheep grazing between Kansas and the flashing Pacific. He tumbles is pulled away from the planet like a caboose waving hilarious goodbyes turns again dives shouting into the pale blue the celestial ocean. Here momentum fails. The parachute blinks open. The trip back down takes hours, and while not as rapturous as the ascent, is by far the best part, the most voluptuous, swinging, floating, architecture of clouds, axe-head cumulonimbus lighting up with vast interior flickers, creamy whites, roiling yellow, streaming grays, black black blacker black, thunder, hail, crackling ganglia of lightning, rain over the city. Ccrab scrapes down on the roof of an apartment building, scuttles across wet tar, unharnesses, looks around. He has to get down through the building, finds a metal door like a slot, goes in. Ccrab descends the dark stairs like a stranger. There are confusions down there, criminals, complications. Ccrab is going to visit his mother. I'm Ccrab. I deal in dreams. This is one to think about.

When I wake up it's morning and I'm in bed next to Cathy June.

"What if you have my baby?" I ask.

"It's not in my horoscope," she reminds me.

In another part of the story some distance away, I see myself in the Plumyth on my way to Hollywood to see Clover Bottom in *My Little Pig*. Plotz and I are supposed to meet Henry Miller at a lecture he's giving at U.C.L.A., but I decide not to go I know it won't work out. He'll want to play ping-pong afterwards I don't want to play ping-pong. He'll want a reading I don't want to give him a reading. He's going to die soon there's nothing I can tell him he doesn't know and what he doesn't know I can't tell him. And besides Durrell is there and he'll get in the way. Henry has some fatherly advice for Plotz, I don't need a father. A mother, maybe.

In the theater lobby I find the refreshment counter, buy three candy bars and a container of popcorn. I stand in the lobby before the film begins looking at still photos of Clover/Cathy June, in this one semi-nude with a man and a woman, in the next with three tough looking adolescents wearing jackets that say *Torrance Tornados*, and finally a close-up of Cathy June's face looking like a hundred other movie stars. Which only goes to show it's the camera man who creates the image not the subject. At one time she was my subject now she's subject to someone else. My fault but unavoidable. How can it be my fault if it's unavoidable. I look at that picture for a long time, slowly eating my popcorn. Kismet. I buy some more popcorn and a coke and walk into the theater.

In the first scene Clover is asleep on the carpet with her teenage boyfriend in an apartment that shows the wreckage of a wild party. The phone rings and it's this guy she meets on her job at the checkout counter of Alpha Beta. "It's the movie producer," she whispers to her boyfriend, holding her hand over the mouthpiece. He wants her to join him and a few friends at his house up in Bel Air where they need someone to perform "an unnatural act" for a few hours. She looks at the clock. "But it's two o'clock in the morning," she says. "That's right," says the guy on the phone.

When I get back to the house it's late afternoon. Leo, who will have disappeared a couple of days ago, hasn't returned. I take a can opener and go outside heading up De Longpré off Hyperion under the blank Los Angeles sky, rattling the can opener. "Pss-pss-pss-pss."

I stop in front of a house with hilly grounds, sniffing and wheezing, the smog is unusually bad today. My eyes are tearing. I peer into a garden of bamboo, palms, pampas grass, avocado trees, bird-of-paradise, most of it a blur to my vision. I can't tell whether it's the smog, the dusk, or my eyes, which have gotten much worse recently.

"Pss-pss-pss-pss," I say, rattling the can opener.

I walk to the other side of the street, gawk up into a monkey puzzle tree, a grove of mimosa.

"Pss-pss-pss-pss." Rattle, rattle.

No response. I stare up over the eucalyptus hiding shabby wooden cottages in the direction of Griffith Park, beyond the neighborhood, above Los Feliz Boulevard. Leo just shows up at my doorstep one day, I always suspect he came from the wilds of Griffith Park. Maybe he will have gone back up there above Los Feelies, as they call it around here.

I see myself around that point taking a drive up to Wang's place in Pacific Palisades. I come in carrying a pizza I pick up on the way. We go out to his patio where I ask for a beer and eat the pizza while talking to Wang.

"What's the matter with you lately?" he asks.

"Meaning what?"

"For one thing your fortunes. The customers are complaining. You're giving them nothing but bad fortunes."

"Kismet," I say.

"Let's leave fate out of it." He pulls some fortune slips out of his pocket. "'Don't make any plans beyond tomorrow.' How would you like that after a light-hearted dinner? 'Be prepared for the big storm.' 'Profit while you can.' 'You are in for a big surprise.' These are fortunes that a party of four got in the Hong Kong last week. They complained to the manager."

"What's wrong with them?"

"They're ominous, that's what's wrong with them. What's wrong with you? You've won. You've sold Cathy June to Drackenstein. You got a finder's fee. You got the money back from him you lost on that campus peace movie flop. You even have a piece of *Pig*. It's just what you predicted."

"The macroconditions conform," I tell him. "The microconditions are always chaotic." I can see him now, stalking through the halls of the Drackenschloss up in Bel Air. He has no aura, Drackenstein, as he opens the door to the bedchamber, he has totally negative vibrations almost as bad as Miracle who sucks everything in like a black hole an energy vampire, that's where they get their power, from others from you and me, we turn them on and once we turn them on there's no turning them off, hypnotizing their victims with an illusion of pleasure, this is going to feel good, and all you have to do is sit there do nothing empty your mind, have a beer maybe while they glut on your vital juices, soul food for that black hole, for that absence that's their essence, that negation, that conduit to nothingness that always has to be filled, she waits in bed, all pink and young, as he slouches to the bathroom to brush his fangs.

"Stop eating that junk Boris, you're going to burst. And forget about her, she was never worth it."

"It doesn't bother me," I tell him. If I happen to tune in when they're making love I go on to other things, that's all. If I have other things to go on to. I usually don't have other things to go on to. Drackenstein goes back to his room after they make love. He doesn't like to sleep with women, they keep him awake. Especially after sex. There's only one way Drackenstein can go to sleep after having sex he masturbates. Then he falls asleep. Except when the moon is full and then he just stays up all night. The full moon is always the most creative time for Drackenstein that's when he gets his best ideas. When the moon is full Drackenstein usually spends the night thinking and jerking off and by morning he often has enough ideas for a whole movie.

"Like hell," says Wang.

"You know the story of Eurydice?" I ask him.

"She gets mixed up with the underworld somehow?"

"They say Miracle is mixed up with the underworld. And Clover's going to get mixed up with Miracle. Then she's going to get mixed up."

"You knew what was going to happen," says Wang.

"When you know what's going to happen you feel like you're playing a part. It feels fake. Part of me wants to play my part out to the end and part of me wants to cut the yarn right here and be done with it."

"Frankly Boris, I think you're having some kind of breakdown. Why don't you come back to the T'ai Chi class? Or call Lazonga. Or get Roxoff."

"Whatever." The sound of the surf makes me dreamy. It becomes the wave breaking, vivid, that we can't see from here, way up above the flashing tilting misting Pacific, hummingbirds, bird-of-paradise, smell of eucalyptus and star jasmine.

*Hello, Boris?* Smell of jasmine, of eucalyptus becomes a sound, becomes a voice. *I can't handle it*, she says, *I'm all strung out.*

*You're getting famous*, I tell her.

*Is that me, or somebody's idea of me?*

"Boris?" says Wang. "Do you ever hear from her?"

"I keep in touch."

I see myself sitting in front of the TV set with a beer, watching the scansion of Clover's image onto the tube.

Clover wears a thin white cotton blouse and tight black velvet jeans. You can see her nipples through the blouse and every time she moves you can watch her breasts nodding yes, shaking no, as if they can't make up their minds. The other guests are fascinated by this indecision and follow every quiver hoping for an answer. The suspense makes them giddy. They laugh at everything, so does the audience. The host exploits the situation.

I can't see what's so funny, says the host. (Laughter.)

That's your hangup. (Laughter.)

Maybe it depends on where he sits.

Did you say *sits*. (Laughter and applause.)

I didn't say zits. (Laughter.) Or pits. Or fits.

I don't know, maybe I should change my seat.

I don't know about you, but I'd like Clover's seat. (Laughter and applause.)

This is getting out of hand, says the host.

Well that's what I say, let's get it in hand. (Laughter and applause.) What's the old saying, two in the hand is worth one in the bush?

Clover laughs with everybody else. She throws her chest out and shakes with laughter, that in itself is enough to steal the show.

Let's be serious, says the host.

Who's kidding?

No, I mean it. I just want to say to Clover that I think she has a beautiful laugh. (Laughter.) Doesn't she have a beautiful laugh? (Laughter and prolonged applause.)

No, seriously, we're not letting Clover get a word in here. She doesn't need to.

No, I mean it Clover, I want to ask you a serious question and I hope you won't take it the wrong way. All of us have seen *My Little Pig*, and if we haven't we should rush right out to see it because it's really a sensational film. Now everyone who sees that film immediately compares you to such superstars as Jane Russell and Marilyn Monroe and Jayne Mansfield. Now they were, frankly, sex stars and they were very up front about it. But as far as I can remember, this is the first time in film history that a sex star is not only up front but also out back. (Laughter and applause.)

So kidding aside, what I want to ask you is, what does it feel like to have the most famous fanny in Hollywood?

It feels good.

I bet it does. (Laughter. Howls. Applause.)

Clover, I wonder if you would be gracious enough to do us a favor. Would you mind standing up and turning around.

Sure.

Clover does as asked and turns around, doing a sassy little bump and grind that could be either provocative or insulting, in fact if her asshole had a tongue, it would probably be sticking out.

There it is folks. Get a closeup of that Freddy. Let's have a big hand for Clover's Bottom, I mean Clover Bottom. And we'll be back in one minute.


Smog. Smog over Hollywood. Smog over Beverly Hills. Smog over Bel Air and Griffith Park. Smog over Pasadena and Santa Monica. Smog over Watts and Torrance, Encino and Van Nuys. Smog over Long Beach and Huntington Beach and Redondo Beach and El Segundo. Smog over Palos Verdes. Smog over the Valley. Smog over San Berdoo. Smog over the San Gabriel Mountains and the Santa Ana Mountains. Smog over Palm Springs and Palm Desert. Smog over Marina del Rey. Smog over the Miracle Mile and the Sunset Strip. Smog over the chic office buildings of Century City. Smog through their revolving doors and up their elevators. Smog through their air conditioning vents and into their offices. And the thickest smog in the offices of Universal International Productions, in the inner office of O.U. Miracle, in conference with Rod Drackenstein and Victor Plotz.

"This won't fly," says Miracle. "The concept is good but we

need something with a stronger simpler story line. A vehicle for Clover, something based more on her personality. What there is of it."

"By personality you mean tits and ass," says Drackenstein.

"I didn't say it," says Miracle. "But this will not sell in Yumpsville. Clover's ass will."

"This is not meant to sell in Yumpsville, O.U. This will sell in New York and L.A. and Paris. This will be a winner in Cannes. This will hit the young hip audience that liked *Blow Up*. This will be an American *Emmanuelle* but with class. It's Fellini making *Deep Throat*."

Miracle pauses before answering. He looks like he's about to pick up a cigar but he doesn't. He looks like he's about to crack a joke but he doesn't. Miracle always looks like he's about to do something he doesn't do, like a man with a pinochle hand tugging lightly at one card, then another till someone grumbles, "Come on, play." What he does is usually a surprise, delivered with an air of good natured malice.

"Look," he says finally. "I don't mean to be impolite, but who do you think you're talking to? I know Fellini as well as you do and you won't get anywhere by being condescending. You still have a chip on your shoulder. Just because you've been screwed. I don't think that's a good reason to put down the industry."

"I want to make one thing clear, O.U. I have absolutely nothing against the pricks who run the movie industry. It's a dirty job and we should all be glad that somebody's doing it."

"Who's playing the Ccrab part?" asks Miracle. "The fortune teller."

"I'm playing the fortune teller. Propper."

"Is that advisable?"

"I can relate to Ccrab. We have similar charts. Besides it's cheaper. Why pay an actor?"

"That's one thing I like about you these days, Rod. You're still cheap. The other thing is that you have Clover. Let's say fifteen bucks, what can I lose? We'll do something a little more toney, all right an update of *The Tempest*, what the hell, it's free. We'll call it *Blown Away*. Sex yes, orgies yes, even incest, but quality. Prestige. Lift it out of the muck. But not too far out. You know what I mean, Victor, by not too far out?"

"Victor will run it through the typewriter again, O.U."

"I hear you," says Miracle.

"Now wait a minute," says Plotz, "What I hear you saying, Rod, is you're not satisfied with my work."

"Cool it, Victor. This is something we can go with, O.U."

"Promise?" Miracle says, looking at Victor.

"By my mother that bored me," says Plotz.

Wake up with a sense of doom. Plotz is dead, dropped dead of a coronary. Just like that. I go out for a paper to look at the obituaries. It's Sunday. There's something else, Leo is still missing. I have to put a lot of coins in the slot for my chunk of the L.A. *Times*, then spend a lot of time paging through the mass of paper to find the obits. Finally there it is. He was fifty, divorced. No kids. He was too young. This hasn't happened yet. It's out of sequence.

On the way back up Hyperion something black at the corner of my eye. I go back. In the gutter. Black. White paws. Long fur. I lift him a little with the point of my shoe to show the white chest. His head falls back against the curb. The only Nepalese in the neighborhood. There's a lot of blood, still slightly viscous. He got to the side of the road at least, and didn't get mashed by the traffic. Let's hope it was quick not bleeding there needing help. He looks peaceful. I tell myself. There's a kind of luminous vapor hovering over him but dissipating fast.

I go back to the house. I'm afraid there are tears in my eyes and thinking of Plotz I feel a little foolish. Go back with a shovel. Spread the "View" section of the *Times* and get him onto it his guts falling out. It must have been quick. Cover him with "Opinion," wrap him in "Home," "Travel," "Outlook," and the "Calendar." Take him back, dig a hole in the patio under the eucalyptus, cover him. He was special. I learned a lot from him. I make a little marker of stones. He was good company.

Philitis will be pacing nervously back and forth while I stare into the crystal ball, cupping my hands on either side of the globe about three inches away. I begin moving them slowly as if caressing its surface. The interior of the glass grows milky. I feel an odd tickling in the forehead just above my nose. Soon the interior of the globe seems to move, to swirl like fog. Bright lights begin to gleam and sparkle, luminous lines, then contours emerge, a scene comes into focus, an interior, the interior of a car, Clover's face in Miracle's lap, his hands under her clothes, Miracle drilling into her the scene goes blurry and disappears.

"What do you see in there," says Philitis, "does it tell you anything?"

"Yes. It tells me I have to split."

"You can't walk out just like that. What am I supposed to do? I spent a year on this project. I'll lose my grant. You agreed . . ."

"I know, I know," I wave him off. "But I can't keep it together any more." I pick up Leo. "Leo's starting to look an awful lot like me, don't you think? He's even beginning to smell like me. Leo's never smelled bad before. And he's developing bags under his eyes like mine, who ever heard of a cat with bags under his eyes?

Listen, if I don't come back, tell Lazonga to take the cat. He's got at least six or seven lives left. Wang can't stand cats, he's too close to a recent cat incarnation."

"What are you talking about Dr. Ccrab? Where are you going? What am I going to do?"

"I couldn't tell you." Philitis' aura is dull grey and jerky. He's going to go into the film industry and make a lot of money but I don't tell him that, he's not ready to believe it. I put Leo down. Strange music fills the air. Leo runs under the sofa.

"Are you planning a trip or what? What's that music?" says Philitis.

"As I said, I'm going to split." I begin to blur and vibrate. A flash of pale yellow dots runs through Philitis' auric pulse, like bubbles through alka seltzer.

"What? what?" he says.

I go out of focus and like an image in a stereoscope start to divide in two. Philitis' eyes go wild, his mouth falls open, his aura pulses like a failing heart. For a moment there are two of me standing side by side. Philitis blinks desperately trying to get us back into focus. Slowly one of me turns and walks out the door, then the other image fades out. A strange gurgling growl comes from under the sofa that starts low and wells higher and louder.

"Dr. Ccrab?" Leo is yowling like a banshee. "Ccrab," Philitis yells, "Holy shit." He staggers out of the bungalow.

Down at the other end of Santa Monica Drackenstein steers the yellow Stingray left from Sepulveda, Plotz resisting his attempts at conversation, then left on Crescent Heights to Laurel Canyon into the hills, Plotz maintaining his silence. Plotz thinks Drackenstein made a big mistake giving in to Miracle about revision, and he knows Drackenstein knows what he's thinking. Drackenstein always has that uncanny ability to guess what you're thinking, he's even sort of famous for it in poker playing circles, so since he knows what I'm thinking, Plotz is thinking, why bother saying it.

"All right, stop sulking Victor," Drackenstein says finally as he steers the car up a winding road off Laurel Canyon.

"You know what I'm thinking. He's going to try to take over the script and besides he'll have final cut so he can always beat you with the editing."

"So what. You're still back in the sixties when there was something to sell out. Now there's nothing to sell. We're just dealing with degrees of crap and our only protection is leverage."

"There is no we anymore," says Plotz. "When there was Miracle was one of us. Back in the sixties. What leverage?"

"Clover is my leverage. You know what a letch he is."

"That's power?"

"Power is anything that gets anybody to do anything."

Plotz taps his forehead. "Watch out for Miracle," he says. "He's a living demonstration of the failure of success."

Drackenkstein pulls in to the carport of a redwood house supported on piano legs over a ravine at one end where the roof slants up high above floor-to-rafter windows and glass doors leading to a deck.

"Don't you ever worry this place is going to collapse in the next quake or mud slide?" asks Plotz.

"That's why they call it Shaky City. Let's go out to the patio."

They go through the living room, its walls collaged with paintings, contemporary unknowns, the kind you could pick up cheap Plotz notes, out to the patio, fuchsia, bougainvillea, star

jasmine, yucca, a few flowering citrus, hummingbird feeder over
the small swimming pool at one end in the sun, a black and
white Persian cat slipping across the flagstones into the shade of
a jacaranda.

"Welcome to the Drackenschloss," says Drackenstein. "How
about a bloody mary?"

"Why not?"

"I've been thinking," says Drackenstein as he brings back the
drinks. "Maybe what we need is to heighten Mandy's sensuality.
We maintain her innocence, but it's a passive, animal innocence.
What do you think? I mean she's not the kind of girl who sits
around playing chess with her boyfriends. And when the jetset
world lands on her desert island she's dazzled by the beautiful
people in it. So Propper thinks he's hypnotized her but she's just
doing what comes naturally. She likes the voluptuousness of
surrender. She likes being the object of everyone's fantasies.
And what about a whiff of incest, I mean they've been alone
together on the island all this time. Then later she begins to
realize how she's being exploited but it's too late, she doesn't
know how to handle it and we have her die at the end."

"I don't know about blowing her away like that Rod."

"Why not?"

"I'm superstitious. The things I write sometimes have a way
of coming true. That's why I've never had anyone die in anything I've written. Let's not open Pandora's box."

"What the hell, Pandora might like it. Besides, you're welcome to your superstitions but this is serious business, we're
dealing with money."

"Anyway your revision, you shouldn't take it as an insult, is a
little vulgar. You're getting right back to the old soft porn

formula you're trying to get away from Rod. Crime doesn't pay, but meantime it's a helluva lot of fun. You're developing an incurable B movie mentality."

"I never said I had anything against vulgarity. I like vulgarity. We're working with a mass medium, there's no place for an alienated elitism here. We have an obligation to the masses."

"You mean the mass market. That's a little different."

"I don't want to think about abstractions now, Victor. We're trying to develop a story."

"What you don't think about you pay for."

"Well, you're being paid for what you don't think about, so let's get on with it." The phone rings. Drackenstein picks up an extension.

"I suppose I'm interrupting something," Claire's voice.

"Excuse me," he says to Plotz, "it's my ex. What makes you think you're interrupting something?"

"Are you alone?"

"No, I'm in conference."

"Really. Who is she?"

"Look, Claire, it's none of your business anymore."

"It never was any of my business. Not even when you started screwing that little slut a month after we got married. The one who ended up in the Vegas whorehouse?"

"Claire, that was seventeen years ago."

"Eighteen."

"How are you getting along. Are you happy?"

"You've got to be kidding."

"All right. What is it?"

"It's your daughter. She's been picked up again."

"Miranda? Where?"

"Calexico. At customs. They found cocaine."

"What the hell was she doing in Calexico?"

"How the hell do I know? Smuggling dope evidently."

"How much?"

"Enough to get her in trouble."

"I'll call Asher."

"Sure. Call the lawyer. Throw some money at it."

"What do you want me to do?"

"Think. Try to think for once in your life instead of evading everything."

"Miranda isn't my fault."

"That's right. Nothing's your fault. Nothing's ever your fault. You better go back to Roxoff. Because there are a lot of things between you and Miranda you still refuse to understand."

"You hate my guts, don't you?"

"You don't have any guts." She hangs up.

"I'll call Asher," says Drackenstein. He puts down the phone.

"Trouble?" asks Plotz.

"I really needed that," says Drackenstein.

"You got divorced five years ago. You're not over it yet?"

"I'm not over my mother yet either," says Drackenstein dialing Asher, who isn't there. He leaves an urgent message.

"What did Dong say?" asks Plotz.

"He says he's tired of doing Orientals."

"Shit, he is an Oriental."

"I pointed that out. He says he's an American. He says you don't have to be Jewish to be an American, even in Hollywood. He wants to do Cal as an Irish revolutionary. He says he doesn't need Hollywood, he has his business. Then he asked for more money and told me to call his agent."

"The hell with him."

"Don't worry he'll do it. Maybe we'll compromise on a Chicano."

Clover comes through the door to the patio wearing silver high heeled evening shoes, red short shorts that expose about a quarter of her buttocks and a no-bra t-shirt that says MOVIE STAR on it.

"Hi sweetheart," says Drackenstein. "You're looking pretty brass ass."

She turns around and gives a wiggle.

"Or should I say sass ass. That could cause a riot in public you know that? How'd you get up here?"

"Roy gave me a lift."

Drackenstein looks pissed. "I thought I told him to stay away from you."

"Oh he's just a boy."

"Don't give me that, he's twenty-one."

"Really. I mean compared to you."

"Who's comparing him to me?"

Roy comes out wearing jeans, work shirt, and straw hat, a squat, husky Spanish kid with a lumpy face.

"You look like a fucking wetback," says Drackenstein.

"Let's not forget I'm a Chicano, Rod."

"You should have thought of that before your bar mitzvah. And cut this 'Rod' shit."

"You're not my real father so I figure it's about time I stop calling you that."

"He suddenly quits Stanford and decides he's a wetback. Chavez raised his consciousness."

"That's right Rod."

"Well raise it a little higher. Twenty years of the best of

everything doesn't add up to Chicano. This state belongs to people like you."

"That's right. You stole it from us."

"How are the Spanish lessons going?"

"Don't put it down. I want to go up to San Juan Bautista and work with El Teatro Campesino, so it's real useful."

"Well that's not a bad idea, but would it be out of the way to suggest that English is even more useful."

"It's useful. We know how to curse you in it."

"Come off it kiddo. You should have rebelled when you were a teen-ager. Like your mishugina sister. Hey what are you doing?"

Clover is pulling off her t-shirt and heading for the pool. Roy's eyes are bugging.

"I'm going for a swim till you guys are finished hassling."

"Knock it off for christsake. I've had it for today. Let's wrap it."

"Maybe you better call Dr. Roxoff," said Plotz.

"What is this with Roxoff today. When I have to see Roxoff I'll know I'm losing it."

"I want to talk to you about the way you treat Mom," says Roy.

"She's not your real mother either, remember? Look I know you got a hardon for Clover, kiddo, but lay off. And I don't really care what you do in the business as long as it's quality."

"Quality is just a code word for white. Maybe it's got something to do with your people, since they run the industry, but it's got nothing to do with my people."

"Gesundheit."

Roy suddenly sneezes.

The same place but eight in the morning. Drackenstein hasn't had a cup of coffee yet. Miracle has a habit of calling him early, it's an assertion of power. He's sitting on his patio in the morning sun on the phone with Miracle about *Blown Away* while watching a hummingbird feeding at the feeder over the pool, an Anna's. He can smell jasmine mixed with citrus blossom in the still chill air as Miracle talks about the "chemistry of this thing. I think we have the right elements here, I know the budget is low but you're good at that Rod, you've done minor miracles with a few bucks. I think we can pull it off. We need the right kind of publicity, the right kind of ad campaign and smart distribution, I'll be thinking about it Rod, that's what I'm good at, I make things happen."

"I'm listening, O.U." A big black and white Persian cat jumps up on Drackenstein's lap, settles in and starts purring.

"I want to go into production right away Rod. Clover's hot. Get on Plotz about that script. Maybe we should have one of my people working with him."

"Don't worry, I'm working with him. It's really my script, he just writes it down."

"Okay I'll leave it to you for the time being. Another thing, I want to get to know your performers a little, I want to get to know their range, their, uh, possibilities. When I present a package I have to know what's in it, that's the way I always work Rod, you know that."

"You mean Clover?" The cat jumps off Drackenstein's lap.

"How about my little place over in Avalon. We could take my seaplane out almost any time. You can come too."

"I'll talk to her about it."

"I mean if she feels like it. I'm not an ogre Rod."

"It doesn't matter whether we're ogres," says Drackenstein. "All that matters is whether we're smart."

"Well we are that Rod, if nothing else. We certainly are smart."

When Miracle hangs up Drackenstein will immediately call Plotz and make an appointment for breakfast. What Miracle doesn't know is that Clover will have ODed on pills last night. Drackenstein still doesn't know whether it's an accident or whether she's depressed or even at the outside whether she's going to recover. And if she recovers what kind of shape she's going to be in. Roy will have found her in the middle of the night next to the pool. He's the one who's been giving her the drugs, Drackenstein doesn't even know she's on anything. They'll have rushed her to the hospital at two a.m. If anybody asks it's being called "exhaustion."

At a light on Sunset on the way down to Beverly Hills Drackenstein notices the license plate of the car in front of him. 2 2 MUCH. He glances in the rear view mirror. The one behind says, Y ME. Drackenstein is real tired of cute license plate graffiti but reflects it's just right the writing in L.A. is on wheels instead of walls. He turns off Sunset down Beverly Drive, corridor of palms alternating tall thin short fat like musical notes, lawns with grass like astroturf. The palms are tree houses for rats, they say. He crosses Santa Monica and little Santa Monica, pulls into a parking lot.

Plotz is already pigging his lox and bagels when Drackenstein walks into Nate 'n Al's. "Have you tried Wheaties?" asks Drackenstein.

"Come on, Rod, it's like Popeye with the spinach. So what are we gonna do? Find a look-alike?"

"Either that or get Ccrab," says Drackenstein. "He knows how to deal with her. As a matter of fact, here's a dime."

Plotz goes and calls Ccrab but gets Lazonga. "Where is he?" asks Plotz.

"He's disappeared," says Lazonga.

"What do you mean he's disappeared? Like Houdini?"

"He had an attack," Lazonga says.

"What kind of attack?"

"I don't know. That's what he called them."

"He had them before?"

"Yes."

"And what happens when he has an attack?"

"He goes rigid. His eyes turn back in his head. He gets very pale. And he stops breathing."

"That's an attack? It sounds more like rigor mortis."

"This one lasted longer than usual. He came over to my house looking very pale and a little incoherent. He said he'd just dropped a c. I said you mean a hundred dollars you've been gambling he said no from his name. He said he'd just split I said from where he said from himself. Then he had an attack."

"Why didn't you call a doctor?"

"He told me not to. He's always come back before."

"So what did you do?"

"I called Wang. He said he'd come over and take care of it. He came over when I wasn't there, Boris seemed stable and I had to go to my job at the bank."

"And?"

"And when he got there Boris had disappeared. At least that's what Wang says."

"And what did you do then?"

"I called the police and filed a missing person report. Why don't you call Wang?"

Plotz finds another dime and calls Wang. "He's finally done it," says Wang.

"Done what?"

"Learned how to become invisible. Nobody's been able to do that since Lamont Cranston. And the real Lamont Cranston went blind and disappeared forever."

"You're shitting me," says Plotz.

"Transmogrified," continues Wang. "That's the rumor."

I don't believe any of this. What happens now?"

"Well," says Wang, "he may reincarnate. Or his astral projection may turn up."

"How will we know which it is?"

"How do we ever know? Who's real and who isn't?" says Wang.

"I never thought about it."

"Well we don't, so what's the difference."

Plotz goes back to the table, orders a scrambled lox and eggs, and tries to explain it to Drackenstein. "It's a metaphor," Drackenstein says finally. "After all he's always been schitzy. He's having an identity crisis. But why does one of him have to become invisible, that's what I find unconvincing."

"Why?" says Plotz. "Lamont Cranston learned how to do it, he did it for years he must have made a million bucks."

"That's right," says Drackenstein. "But while The Shadow's become immortal they say the real Lamont Cranston went blind and disappeared forever."

"He should have tried a new agent," Plotz says. "Speaking of invisible, there's Ronni over there, she's been invisible for years."

"I heard she had a breakdown," says Drackenstein.

"Schitzo scherzo. Also known as exhaustion. They say Cranston transmogrified, that's the rumor. So anyway," says Plotz.

"So anyway what's going to happen with Ccrab?"

"I don't know," says Plotz. "He may come back. This has happened to him before. Or his astral projection may turn up."

"How will anyone know which it is?"

"How do we ever know? Who's real and who isn't? I've thought for a long time that Miracle isn't real. I think he's just an intersection of market forces, like a kind of moral hologram, but I couldn't prove it."

"Anyway," says Drackenstein, "we've got to find Ccrab. Either one of him. Or both of him. I don't care which. He sold us on her, he's responsible for her."

"Maybe we can return her and get our money back," says Plotz.

It will seem like yesterday he last saw Cathy June. Time is a way of perceiving that psychics often ignore. Think sideways. Crab in the Plumyth chugging up the steep winding roads of Bel Air. I'm Ccrab, the omniscient narrator. I am I. He is me. Where ego I go. Crab drives past palaces hedged and fenced, ranch and Roman, Tudor and Spanish, Frank Lloyd modern and Disney gothic, Bauhaus and whorehouse, dusk rising and the lights of the city spreading behind. It's dumb but it's beautiful, he'll muse. He'll stop at a high iron gate the motor overheating as a spotlight goes on. "Please speak your name into the receiver," a metallic baritone will announce from a post next to the car. "B.O. Crab," I hear him saying, reflecting that security's tightened up since Manson. The gate will swing open he drives in, up a winding road dimly visible in the beam of the one headlight for about five minutes to a gravel parking area where he parks the smoking Plumyth among a silver Bentley a maroon Mercedes an orange Lincoln two Porsches a pink Eldorado convertible a Volvo P-1800 in mint condition a red Jaguar sedan a bright yellow Stingray and an old beat green Dodge pickup truck. He walks up a gravel path among well lit lawns to a pillared portico where a door will be opened by a footman in uniform who points across a vast entrance hall along which he hikes to another door attended by another footman into the "library," a very large room with no books a gothic look Renaissance paintings a huge Persian rug and an enormous fireplace flickering at the other end, like an imitation of one of the imitations in Hearst Castle, the scale dwarfing the ten or twelve people gathered near the massive hearth though there are among them in fact several of substantial worldly and even psychic stature, including Wang and Lazonga, whose brains Miracle is storming for the film. An Oscar stands on the high mantel, golden calf of the industry. The Miracle mansion is the legacy of O.U.'s father, Miles Miracle, who built the Miracle Mile. Strange sourceless music drifts through the chamber in Crab's wake. "Aloha-a-a-a!" Wang yowls, already juiced.

Crab will have been summoned there by Drackenstein. Getting back to his bungalow on Hyperion, he finds the telegram from Drackenstein: CATHY JUNE IN TROUBLE NEED YOU AT MIRACLES. He comes immediately, even after all these months of separation enforced by Drackenstein during her rocketing rise to fame as Clover Bottom. Crab knows Clover's problem is Drackenstein, and he has some plans in mind for Drackenstein. Crab has changed his mind, now he has to change Drackenstein's. Crab knows he's made a mistake even though it's a mistake he had to make. Now he's going to try to save Clover from that mistake by converting Drackenstein from insentience to consciousness. It will be a disaster for Drackenstein's career. I'm Ccrab, I've given up, I'm just telling you what will happen, the teller without fortune, while Crab, still trying, remains the unfortunate fortune teller.

When Crab gets to talk with Clover, whom he hasn't seen since she was Cathy June Grunion, she smiles at him a little guiltily and kisses him on the cheek. "So you see it all came true," she says.

"And did they all live happily ever after?"

"Truly. This one got a little strung out."

"What about Cathy June."

"Cathy June's split. I'm Clover."

"Might be a good idea to keep in touch."

"She doesn't exist anymore."

"What is this power Drackenstein has over you?" asks Crab.

"I need someone around who can define me," says Clover.

"You're already defined. You're Clover Bottom."

"I know, it really blows me out. I mean one of the best things I like about being in the movies is meeting movie stars. I want to ask for their autographs all the time but Rod says it's not cool. Now people ask for my autograph and I go, You want *my* autograph?"

Roy Drackenstein puts a heavy disco number on the stereo and starts dancing with Clover. In her rhinestone studded sweater and tight black leather pants, Clover is possessed with a wild, undulant energy. She looks like a flash of hope, a flame flicking loose from its wick. Miracle asks Roy to turn it off so Dudley Avis can do a song.

"Sing something for us, Dudley." Avis picks up his guitar, singing:

Going off the deep end
On a crazy weekend
It's the way to go
If you want to flow
If you want to change
And be rich and strange
Going off the deep end . . .

Meanwhile Roy Drackenstein pursues his crude designs on Clover with the mocking aid of Dong Wang.

"You sure you want this?" asks Wang.

"It works?" asks Roy.

"Sure it works. What do you think."

"Then I want it."

Wang shrugs. "Okay. But be careful. It's powerful stuff." He pulls a small paper bag out of his pocket and hands it to Roy. Roy opens it and takes out a vial of red liquid.

"This is it? What's in it?"

"Damiana, amyl nitrate, ginseng, coke, estrogen, amphetamine, spanish fly and so on. A little this, a little that."

"You get good results?"

"I never use it myself. Unpredictable side effects."

"Like what?"

"Oh. Frenzy. Depression. Rage. Nymphomania."

Lazonga catches up with Crab looking indignant. Clara is a double Virgo and you know what that means. "You ought to be ashamed at what you're doing to that girl," she snaps at Crab.

"Me?"

"You. Boris Crab."

"They're doing it. I'm not doing anything."

"You're all doing it. Let's be precise. You did hand her over to Drackenstein, didn't you?"

"That was her karma. You can't rewrite somebody's story."

"Look here C.c. What you're doing is presiding over the destruction of that girl's identity."

"Identity? We're all more or less interchangeable Clara. Besides, she's already a split personality. She and Cathy June are two different people."

"Split baloney, C.c. That girl's consciousness is so underdeveloped there's nothing to split."

"Well why don't you talk to her Clara."

"That I will do C.c. And meantime maybe you can manage to keep your claws off her."

"I don't know if I can promise you that Clara. It depends more on her than on me."

"You're such a Cancer. You think you're still in love with her. I know you C.c. You could fall in love with your shoe if your imagination started working on it."

"You ought to know Clara."

"Don't go hangdog on me again C.c. I have nothing against you. I'm extremely fond of you. It's just that I don't need men anymore. Except occasionally. I've had my Boston Tea Party and I've thrown it all overboard." *You're still rather attractive*, she's thinking.

*I'm not in the mood now I can't think of making love to anyone else*, Crab thinks.

*I miss you a lot sometimes.*

*I do too maybe we can get it together again when this is all over it can't be long.*

*Maybe for a while it won't last too bad besides when this is all over you won't be in any shape.*

*You may be right you may be right hold me I need it.*

*We both need it we both need a recharge my dear come.*

She holds out her arms, they embrace, they stand that way eyes closed holding one another for a long time.

Meanwhile, Roy will have administered Wang's love potion to Clover in a glass of coca-cola and is hovering around her waiting for results. She's huddled in front of the hearth looking miserable, staring into the fire. Suddenly Crab realizes he can read her mind again. *Onions every time I peel a layer inside me there's another layer it won't stop till there's nothing left.* He notices tears streaking her face in the firelight.

"What are you crying about?" he asks her.

"Everything," she says. "I'm bummed out."

"You can always take your fuck-you money and walk out," says Crab, knowing very well what her answer will be: To what?

"To what?" answers Clover. Roy makes a clumsy attempt to caress her shoulder but she shrugs him off without even looking up. Miracle comes over and gives him a real hard look.

"Jerk off," says Miracle.

Roy turns red. "I was just," he says.

"Is this kid giving you trouble honey?" asks Miracle. "Maybe you'd like to lie down somewhere."

"Why don't you use my cloak?" Crab suggests to Drackenstein. "She looks chilly." Drackenstein grabs Crab's cloak and walks over to the fireplace. "Clover's just a little cold, aren't you baby?" He wraps her up in the cloak and gives her a hug.

"What's the problem?" asks Miracle.

"She's not feeling well, I'll take care of it," says Drackenstein. He kisses her on the forehead, she suddenly responds with her mouth, pulls him down to her, practically wrestles him to the floor. Crab feels a cadenza of jealousy subside into the basso throb of despair. Drackenstein leads her out of the library, out through labyrinthine halls, complicated apartments, empty rooms toward the dark shrubbery of the grounds. By the time they reach the portico she's pushing him beyond the curtain of light, rolling him down onto the damp lawn, smothering him in her breasts, making him suckle, tearing at his clothes, taking him in her mouth, grabbing his balls, pulling him into a riptide of pleasure.

That night Drackenstein dreams that his penis is dripping blood.

Crab is having a lot of eye trouble. That's because he has a lot of I's. I'm Ccrab. I'm the omniscient narrator. Crab's eyes don't converge anymore. When he looks at things he has multiple vision. He sees images at a variety of temporal distances, beginning with here, also known as now, and extending to back there, up ahead, and over to the side. In fact the very idea of direction is becoming ambiguous for him, not to mention here and now. He sees things others don't and doesn't what they do. His friends think he's gone off the deep end, they never know whether to believe him anymore. All this comes about because he's in a transitional state. Very fluid. There's another Crab who is more disengaged, who can see more of what's going on because he's less involved, he's hardly there, a vague embodiment, passing from visibility to invisibility from body to body taking possession like a loa, a spirit. He's less interested in given destinies than Crab, including his own, he has more authority. That's because he's closer to me. I'm Ccrab. I'm the omniscient narrator. The Father, the Son, and the Holy Ghost was basically the solution to a narrative problem.

I'm Ccrab. I'm the omniscient narrator. I know what Crab has in mind. He's going to try to "inhabit" Drackenstein in order to influence him. This kind of habitation often has the effect of breaking down a personality into its component parts. There's a good Drackenstein and a bad Drackenstein. There's an ambitious Drackenstein and a death-wish Drackenstein. There's a vindictive Drackenstein and a forgiving Drackenstein. There's a power Drackenstein and a love Drackenstein. There's a crazy Drackenstein and a normal Drackenstein. And that's not all. Drackenstein used to be a rickshaw boy in Shanghai. He used to be a railroad baron with mystical inclinations. He used to be a flamenco dancer in Granada. He used to be a blacksmith in seventeenth century England. He used to be one of the wives of a Bedouin chief who was abducted and killed in a tribal raid. He used to be a giraffe in the Kalahari hunted by pygmies with poison darts. He's going to be a holy beggar in a dusty Himalayan village. Among other things.

Plotz was the stillborn son of a bad English novelist. He's going to be the wife of a wheat collective officer in the Ukraine. After bearing six children he'll die of childbirth complications attributable to malnutrition during a catastrophic drought. Lazonga was an eminent Jewish physician in the Levant who practiced Kabbalah. She's going to be a great Russian poet, also known for his prowess as a long distance runner. Dong was eaten by the Donner party after which he became a Persian cat. Then he was a machinist. He's going to be a violinist. Miracle in a karmic sense isn't yet real. He's a meta-person. He was synthesized out of the culture, a sort of assemblage. He's very old and will live a very long time at the end of which he will not transmigrate but simply evaporate.

Crab was a sailor, a thief, a mother of four, a condottiere, a cat, a spider, a seamstress, an insurgent, a father of multitudes, a fish, a pianist, a praying mantis, a pimp, a shaman, a red shafted flicker, a toad, an amoeba, a dervish, a sex fiend, a dermatologist, a madame, a madman, a rabid bat. He's going to be a rabbi. I'm Ccrab. But not for long. In her last incarnation Clover was a caterpillar. She's going to be reborn a samoyed. She's one of the karmic underdogs, it's only through a kind of fluke that she got to be a human this time around. It would take a miracle to give her another chance, a chance nevertheless for which her spirit yearns.

"It turns out Mandy's just a dummy, right?" I hear Plotz saying. They're having a plot conference. "Once she gets off the island she can't think of anything better to do than become a go-

go dancer, strictly Las Vegas. But as soon as she gets in front of a camera she goes into a trance and brings back the spirit of a dead movie goddess, what do you say Professor?"

"It's possible," says Crab. "In principle there's only one sex goddess, periodically called up from the underworld in the person of yet another doomed avatar. The Director as necromancer, sustaining dead spirits with blood rites. He drains her till she becomes a completely empty medium for his own evil schemes. It's a traditional vampire theme."

"Terrific," says Drackenstein. "She becomes a walking zombie. And the question is can she throw off the spell."

"And the answer is no," says Plotz.

"Of course she can't," says Drackenstein. "She's doomed from the start."

"Shit. Shit. Shit. It'll be another *Black Orpheus*," says Plotz.

"Oh Christ. Only white," says Drackenstein.

Crab catches Drackenstein's eye and holds it. *On the other hand we don't want another degrading role for Clover.*

"But on the other hand," says Drackenstein, "we don't want another degrading role for Clover. We're trying to upgrade the operation. Quality. Uplift."

"Is this Rod Drackenstein I hear talking?" says Plotz.

"Maybe we can even think in terms of the Eurydice myth," says Drackenstein, "you know where Morpheus is trying to save her from the underworld. I mean something with a little spiritual resonance."

"That's Orpheus. What do you know about the Orpheus and Eurydice myth?" says Plotz.

"I don't know. I never heard of it before," says Drackenstein. "I got a headache. You two work it out," he says.

"Yeah, don't worry Rod," says Plotz. "We'll figure something out."

"Right," says Drackenstein. "Just keep thinking about the chumps in Yumpsville."

"That sounds more like Rod Drackenstein," says Plotz.

"Let's take a break," says Crab. "I'm exhausted." He can see Crab departing Drackenstein's body like an exhalation, like cigarette smoke.

I'm getting fragments of a scene over in Chaplin's office. Like hearing yourself on tape. Media schitz. Everyone becoming everyone. Miracle Plotz Drackenstein are meeting about the film in Charlie Chaplin's old office over on La Brea off Sunset. Lots of wood, mementos of Chaplin, many pictures of the great man hung on the paneled walls. "Nice, huh?" says Miracle. "We acquired it from Herb Alpert. Try to keep it the way Chaplin had it. We want to identify with his identity. The town is full of personalities now but no real identities. There are two things about his career that I admire. The idea of artists controlling their own professional lives that resulted in United Artists. And the way he provided quality entertainment for the masses."

"It also resulted in his permanent exile from America," says Drackenstein.

"What he did we no longer can do," says Miracle. "But we can do other things."

"That's right," says Plotz. "We can make money."

Miracle glowers at him as if he's about to hurl a thunderbolt, but he doesn't. Instead he looks him up and down and says, "What have you got on your feet, for christ sake? Thom McAn? Why don't you get yourself a decent pair of shoes?" He offers Plotz a cigar. "We get them from Cuba. Maybe we'll get back there some day. Meantime there's Vegas. We keep making tactical reappraisals," continues Miracle, who likes to expound. "In the sixties it was the youth culture now it's something else, so what. Just keep your eye on the ball and don't leave anything to chance. The weak need chance, the powerful have other resources. Isn't that right Rod?"

"Let's be realistic," says Drackenstein. "We manufacture a product. It's as real as coca-cola."

"Reality is always elsewhere," Plotz says.

"There you go again, Victor," says Miracle. "Everything is real in the long run so let's forget about it. We're masters of the obvious. And speaking of the obvious, the idea I want to run by you has the inevitability of revealed truth. What would you say, Victor, to writing a novel out of the production as we go along."

"The script isn't finished yet," says Plotz.

"So it'll be a prenovelization. It'll be a terrific promotion gimmick, and it can be sold on the basis that it will soon be a major motion picture."

"Fine, but suppose the film turns out to be real different from the novel?"

"Better," says Miracle. "Then we can do a renovelization based on the film. We'll have three products instead of one. What do you say?"

"Sure, if it pays," says Plotz.

"It pays," says Miracle. "What do you think, I'd ask you to do it on spec? One thing though. The whole project has to be based on Clover's personality, because as we all know, the only role she can play is herself. And the trouble is she tells me the character Mandy in the script doesn't seem like herself anymore."

"Well we have a problem there, O.U., in that she doesn't have much of a self," says Drackenstein.

"Besides," says Plotz, "reading about yourself is always a bummer. It's like hearing yourself on tape or seeing yourself on TV. It never seems like your self to yourself. That's because your self from the outside isn't yourself. It's a third person, a him. All media induces schizophrenia, or what we used to call schizophrenia. Now multiple personality is becoming the norm. Everyone is becoming everyone. And no one."

"Include me out," says Miracle.

"People like you and Rod are old fashioned. So am I. Our whole lives are directed toward becoming somebody. For us when someone fails he becomes nobody and being nobody is something we can't tolerate. That's because we want to suppress the fact that everybody becomes no body in the long run."

"Did you hear about the Polish starlet who fucked the writer, Victor?" says Miracle. "Just make sure the prenovelization is a quick read. A catastrophe story. What happens after the big storm. Shakespeare in La La Land. Blown Away. If you can't tell me about it in one sentence I don't want to hear it."

The day before, Drackenstein picks up Plotz outside his house in Brentwood, "the closest thing I could find to Queens in La La Land."

"What's the best way out to Watts from here?" asks Drackenstein.

"Probably the San Diego to the Santa Monica to the Harbor. Why are we going to Watts?"

"Because I want the real L.A. in this film. The real L.A. is Rosemead. Bell Gardens. Bellflower. Monte Bello. El Monte. Buena Park. Artesia. Reseda. Gardena. Tarzana. Sherman Oaks. La Mirada. Costa Mesa. Canoga Park, places like that. Watts. The ghetto is part of the real L.A. The Watts Towers, I'm thinking of using it as a location."

"That big Coney Island looking monstrosity? It reminds me of Luna Park. Where did you get that idea?"

"I got it from Crab. He told me all about the Watts Towers. It's the realest thing in Los Angeles. It's made from the bricks, the tiles, the old tin cans, the debris of the city itself. And it was made by an ordinary working man in his spare time, not as a work of art, but because, he said, he wanted to do something for the people. There aren't that many things that are worth doing, when you come down to it. Those things must be a hundred feet high."

"Miracle isn't going to like this."

"We're not going to tell him. This guy Rodia, he was an anarchist of some kind. He must have had fun doing it because he worked at the towers for thirty-three years. And when he was done he just walked away and never came back, did you know that? Left the whole thing to a neighbor who didn't know what the hell to do with it. It almost makes me weep. The man was a real artist Victor. Died in poverty up north somewhere."

"Exactly what scene were you thinking of doing there?"

"Well I was thinking of sort of a new scene where we make it clear that Propper is basically bananas. Maybe he has a fight with his gofer Harry, for example, and climbs up one of the towers screaming about how he's not a sorcerer he's just a fake?"

"Christ, what is this, *The Hunchback of Notre Dame?*"

"Well listen, you can fit it into the script, you're the writer. I just want to use the location."

"Who's going to do Harry?"

"I think we're going to get Dudley Avis."

"Miracle's gay friend. He can't act he's a real mouth breather."

"Casting is my business Victor. Besides, he's cheap. And we get the increment of his being Miracle's protegé."

"That's not increment. That's excrement."

But Drackenstein will not be listening. He's worrying. He doesn't feel like himself lately. Or he feels like another self, one less sure of itself. Some of the feelings he's been having lately seem quite alien to him, sentimental, morbid, self-defeating. He feels himself becoming too dependent on Clover, is getting addicted to sleeping with her. Even his dreams seem strange, uncharacteristic, as if he's suffering from some kind of dream invasion. He's sure his meditation on his role as the fortune teller in the film has something to do with it, as well as his conversations with Crab on the characterization, as if his effort to empathize with that personality, so different from his own, has opened up a gap in himself through which another Drackenstein is struggling to emerge, a Drackenstein he does not want to encourage. And yet Crab will have assured him that their horoscopes are almost the same. Only yesterday he will have gone to visit Lazonga in Venice to improve his zodiacal comprehension of the Crab role. But Lazonga refuses to do anything except read his tea leaves, saying she doesn't want to make any long term analyses.

After he drinks the tea she serves, Lazonga instructs him to swing the cup around three times in his left hand. She then takes the cup from him and stares into it for several minutes, turning it this way and that while muttering and gesticulating. Finally she looks up and says, "Very interesting."

"Well?" says Drackenstein.

"The pattern is completely doubled. You have a lily at the top of the cup, which means health and happiness, and one at the bottom, which means anger and strife. You have a dog at the top of the cup, which means faithful friends, and one at the bottom, which means secret enemies. In the middle you have a mushroom, which means sudden separation, and a razor, which means separation in love. On the other hand a harp and a frog indicating love, and the number two. Two anchors clear and cloudy, meaning success in business and failure in business. You have a mountain on the left, meaning powerful friends, and many mountains on the right, meaning equally powerful enemies. This fortune indicates break-up, separation, disintegration, both for better and for worse. To begin very soon, perhaps already begun. Love will be bad for business and business for love. You cannot be both captain of your fate and master of your soul. Only death resolves all contradictions."

And in fact Drackenstein is brooding about death lately, a fact that surprises him, first of all that he should be brooding, and second that he should be brooding about death. Yet he is at an age, is he not, when we sometimes think of death, that cancels everything out finally, as Crab tells him, as if it never happened, he thinks, as they drive up to the Watts Towers, and maybe it doesn't, as Crab likes to speculate, he thinks, or maybe it happens in some other way, a way that strikes you at that last moment as your head falls back against the pillow, fighting for breath, that last moment as you drown and as they say your whole life unreels in an instant, projected on the screen of your mind. And maybe you realize then that none of it has happened yet, till that very last cut, he thinks, when the final vision, version, when the shape of the whole thing occurs to you. Or maybe what occurs to you is that there is no final version, that it was all a dream, or like a dream, but what is a dream like, doesn't a dream also really happen. And what does it mean to happen, as Crab likes to ask, is this happening now as he stands regarding the eccentric reality of the Watts Towers, a gaudy materialization of the city's junk, its neon and tacky glamour, of it not about it, insinuating by its presence that the city really exists. Or maybe death is the only thing that really happens and the rest is collective invention, history a turgid little drama amidst the intergalactic silences. Segue to nothing.

In any case, Drackenstein is lately haunted by many ghosts amorous and familial, ghosts of others, ghosts of himself, clamoring in his head with claims that seem more authentic than his own and that seem irreconcilable in their contradictions. He'll get home that evening to find Roy dancing with Clover in the living room, and will watch without interrupting them the expression of wild pleasure on Clover's face as she moves to the loud, heavy beat, and the splendid vitality of the way she moves. Roy, Drackenstein knows, is irritated by Clover's constant presence at the Drackenschloss. He thinks that if she's going to be living there she should be sleeping with him instead of with Rod. And in fact they are about the same age, they have a lot of the same interests, and inevitably spend a lot of time together. Drackenstein has to keep an eye on them all the time and keeps giving them oblique lectures on self control. Clover's such a horny woman sometimes Drackenstein thinks she'll make love with anyone who rubs her the right way and Roy is still full of uncontrollable adolescent lust. Meantime Miracle is dropping a hint a day about how he expects Clover for a visit out at his "little place in Avalon" and the more Drackenstein puts him off the more he imposes his own ideas on the film.

Drackenstein lets them dance and takes a walk around the grounds, going "psss-psss-psss" behind every bush and fruit tree. On top of everything else, the cat has been missing for several days and when he asks Crab about it, he's supposed to be a psychic after all, he refuses to tell him anything but his expression indicates the worst.

Drackenstein is worried about Clover's roller coaster moods, alternating between highs and depressions. They're going into production now and Drackenstein doesn't know whether she can get through it. He's usually good at manipulating his actors, but if he starts falling in love with Clover forget it, and he feels an unforeseen drift toward the edge. The edge of a water fall, that's one way to put it, a water fall of passion, along with an inertia, a lack of will to do anything about it.

Then, speaking of ghosts, he'll get a call from his ex-wife, Claire, the other day from Carmel, that their daughter has been bailed out by Asher and is now up there with her in terrible shape and wants to come down to Los Angeles. Miranda, whom he and Claire named after the Supreme Court's famous Miranda decision in the days when they were both heavily involved in civil liberties causes, is a high school dropout who goes to live in a commune in the Nevada desert, and when it breaks up drifts into Las Vegas where she becomes an occasional go-go dancer and god knows what else. At this point he will not have seen her for two years, another ghost, the last time is at his mother's funeral back east, his mother and father, more ghosts.

Drackenstein will go to bed early that evening and alone. Clover stays up with Roy who's teaching her how to play chess. He says she's surprisingly good at it once she learns the rules. Drackenstein approves. It will be good for her mind and Roy's glands. He's aware that one of the reasons for her emotional instability is her lack of intellectual resources. Crab will not have helped much since being asked to act as Clover's advisor. It's assumed he has a certain amount of power over her, but mostly he just seems more visible. Though the connection between visibility and power should be obvious, especially to people involved in the electronic media. Drackenstein knows that the invisible are ghosts, they're simply not part of history, and bringing their voices back into reality usually requires something like blood sacrifice, a riot, a war, a revolution, and even then what you get from them mostly amounts to slobber and gibberish.

What Drackenstein doesn't know is that he is gradually being inhabited by the invisible in the persona of Crab, a metamorph of Crab only partly under Crab's control. As Crab will at this very moment be explaining to Dong, a large part of Clover's rehabilitation consists of Drackenstein's habitation by a metamorphic spirit, an entity which, once embodied, will also serve to disseminate Crab's spirit after he will have disappeared from the scene.

Suddenly, stiff as a bullet Drackenstein feels himself shot straight into the air. So fast it feels like slow he rockets up spurting through the first layer of clouds with a soft plop the air grey then mustard then pink plunging into the celestial ocean blue as time and he's free soaring like a shark gaining momentum till there's no such thing as speed or motion everything happening at once he tumbles away from the planet like a caboose then slows, pauses, the parachute blinks open, fills, milky white and pink at the tip. The trip back down takes hours, floating, swinging, voluptuous, architecture of clouds, axe-head cumulonimbus lighting up with vast interior flickers, creamy whites, roiling yellow, streaming greys, black black blacker black, thunder, hail, crackling ganglia of lightning, rain over the city. Drackenstein scrapes down on a roof as the chute collapses, he unharnesses himself. He has to get down through the building, finds a narrow door like a slot, penetrates its darkness. He descends the stairs cautiously, like a stranger. There are confusions down there, criminals, creeps, complications. Drackenstein is going to visit his mother.

He wakes up it's morning, he's in bed next to Clover.

"What if you had my baby?" he asks.

"I'm not the mother type," she says.

Meanwhile the plot conferences are hell. Plotz doesn't care about the film, he's just doing his job. Crab keeps insisting that everybody express their real feelings about the story, he figures that's the best way to sabotage it. Plotz keeps insisting he doesn't have any real feelings about the story. Plotz says that if he had any real feelings about the story he wouldn't be writing it. On the rare occasions when somebody starts getting a workable idea Crab gives him the evil eye and he flounders and loses conviction. "Well, it was just an idea." Plotz keeps arguing with Crab about technicalities on the basis of his research. According to Plotz you absolutely have to draw a circle and sacrifice a chicken if you want to call up a spirit. Crab, of course, insists that the stage decoration is all hype. Plotz says Madame Blavatsky and Aleister Crowley. Crab tells him he's a formalist. He calls Crab inauthentic. Drackenstein says if he wants to call up a spirit all he needs is the number of a casting agency, and that they should get it straightened out. This goes on for two days.

Then Miracle gets the idea it should be a snuff film. He says he knows where he can get the footage. He gets to Drackenstein who thinks it's a great idea as long as it's legal. Crab calls Drackenstein and tells him it won't be GP, it won't even be X. Miracle calls Drackenstein and says he knows damn well that violence is never X only sex is X. Drackenstein says they can have a snuff scene as long as it's GP. Plotz says you can't have a snuff scene without sex, it'll ruin the plot. Drackenstein says they can have a snuff scene with sex if it has redeeming social value. That holds everything up for a week. Finally Plotz comes up with Clover abducted by a cult of ghouls and sex maniacs who sincerely believe that blood sacrifice can end a drought. Crab says it's formula stuff right out of *Tarzan* and *King Kong*. Drackenstein says he has nothing against formulas when they make millions of dollars and that Crab is only a technical advisor who should leave questions of art to those who know about them. He also says that "abductions are very in. Patty Hearst," he says. He tells them to think about what happened in that closet.

I can't help noticing that at the beginning of the cycle Ccrab was the heavy but that this time around it's Drackenstein who's the heavy and Crab will be the good guy. I'm Ccrab. Maybe it doesn't matter so much who you are as where you're at.

On that particular day, Crab will go back to his bungalow lonely and depleted with the effort to sustain his identity, feeling as if he were impersonating himself, and will find Leo waiting for him on his doorstep. That morning Drackenstein will have awakened with a headache after a flying dream that ends with him parachuting down on a rooftop. While he's having coffee Crab calls to complain about Miracle's latest cockamamie idea about the script. Drackenstein blows up and tells Crab he's only a technical advisor who should leave questions of art to those who know about them. Besides, he tells Crab, "abductions are very in. Patty Hearst. Think about what happened in that closet." He hangs up. He feels like letting everything go to hell, including the film. But after breakfast his better self emerges. He calls Roxoff. The secretary says he's in the middle of a group therapy session but he comes to the phone anyway.

Drackenstein explains where he thinks Clover is at.

"I never prescribe over the phone," he tells Drackenstein. "I can give her an appointment."

"She doesn't want to go see you because she says you try and hit on her."

"What the hell, let it all hang out, all she has to do is say no. I mean when I see her that's a factor, everybody with a putz wants to hit on Clover. Okay look, the thing about Clover is she's got a Eurydice complex."

"Which is?"

"When she was pre-pubescent she had an encounter with a child molester in this place out in Downey called Dennis the Menace Park. It's the first erotic experience she remembers and she never told anybody. Later on the guy became a famous rapist known as "The Menace of Dennis the Menace Park," she recognized his picture when they caught him. She's got an immense amount of guilt attached to sex plus a need to be passive, taken advantage of. Typically she has two men in her life, one who puts her through hell, exploits her, makes her feel as worthless as she knows she is, the other who keeps trying to save her and fails. Pluto and Orpheus. You're Orpheus."

"Lucky me."

"Look if you want my advice, cut out. She's hopeless. And if you decide to split, give me her phone number."

"Thanks. I'll keep it in mind."

"Don't mention it. I'll send you a bill."

Drackenstein is feeling sorry for himself. He feels like a billiard ball, hitting on people and going off on his way in the

cold geometry of social encounters you learn to accept after your
first divorce when you realize that no relations are permanent.
Even my cat's gone, he thinks. He gets out a recording he will
have made of a phone conversation with his parents in New
York just before they died so he'll always be able to call them up.
He calls them often at the time, because retired, their children
gone, their families dead, their friends also or moved away, they
see almost no one, know almost no one. They give the impression of people who have long outlived their lives, through luck
or misfortune or some stubborn and unwanted vitality, improbable survivors of a stable middle class whose solidity, with all its
problems, had been unproblematic. His contact with that world
is only through them, and his contact with them, as with most
other realms that don't involve a project or a love affair, consists
largely of encounters with electronic apparitions whizzing
through the ether, disembodied voices or images, the kind of
images he himself creates and vends. He mixes a bloody mary
and takes it and the tape recorder out to the patio. As he presses
the button to begin the mournful ritual the pool, the hummingbird feeder, the colorful flowers, the semitropical greenery all
seem slightly fake, a stage set for a dialogue among clamoring
ghosts.

> Hello? Mother's faint voice.
> Hi, how are you?
> Who is it?
> It's me.
> Who?
> Rod, your son. Remember me?
> Oh. Yes. Where are you?
> I'm in California. As usual.

Oh, California. There haven't been any earthquakes?

Well, there was one in Japan a few weeks ago.

In Japan? Are you all right?

It didn't do much damage in Beverly Hills. So how are you?

I don't know. How's Miranda?

She's fine. What's wrong?

She sighs, a sigh Drackenstein recognizes well, that imposed a metric on his childhood.

Is there anything I can do?

It would be nice to see you.

I plan to fly in soon. Maybe next month. How's Dad?

He still has pain. He can't sleep, he can't eat. The doctor says there's nothing to do.

Can you go out?

Where are we going to go? You can't get a cab. If you go out in the street you get mugged. And who are we going to see? Everybody's dead.

I don't know what to tell you. Let me say hello to Dad a minute.

There's a pause during which he can hear the sound of a sports announcer, then Drackenstein's father gets on the phone. Howya doin' kid? Voice of the old jock, he thinks. When are you going to get a haircut?

I just got one. Mother says you're not so hot.

Just a little pain. So what? A little pain never hurt anyone.

Are you doing anything for it?

There's nothing you can do about it. There are some things in this world you just can't do anything about. Pain is pain, it's nothing to worry about. There's an expression, grin and bear it.

What's wrong with mother she sounds so down?

Nothing. Your mother is always down, that's just the way she is. But she was just talking to your brother on the phone, you know, that always gets her goat.

What's the trouble with Marty?

Eh. Same old thing. Your brother is very impractical. He's too good for his own good. All he wants to do is read and write and he can never make a nickel. Listen, this is costing you money. Besides, I'm listening to the game.

Okay, let me say goodbye to Mother. And take it easy.

Righto. Keep punching.

His mother gets back on the phone. Listen, maybe you could give Marty a call? she asks.

How come?

I don't know, he's just lost his job again, maybe you can give him some advice.

I'll give him a ring. Maybe he can give me some advice. He usually does. Where is he?

He's still in Oklahoma City. He's home now, I just talked to him.

Okay, I'll call him right away. Take care of yourself. Stay warm. Goodbye.

Goodbye, goodbye.


Drackenstein turns off the recorder and looks through his phone file for his brother's number. As he looks he finds himself sighing, and realizes the family sigh is a lot like a breathing technique Roxoff taught him for "getting things off his chest." The whole family has a talent for letting things go after a certain point anyway, a kind of worldly suicide, a summary fuck it all. Of this tendency his twin brother is the purest family example, which is probably why he's an artist, if that's what he is, since as far as Drackenstein knows he never produced any art. He finds a number for him in Bismarck, North Dakota.

"Hello, Marty?"

"What's the occasion? Wait, you were listening to the tape where Mom says you should call me up, right? Well I'm working, I'm solvent, I got a poetry in the schools gig for three months. So is there anything else to talk about?"

"We could say hello."

"Hello."

"So what are you going to do next."

"Something will turn up."

"How do you get these jobs anyway, since you haven't published any poetry?"

"I'm recognized."

"What do you mean recognized?"

"People recognize me."

"You mean they recognize you for the essential artist you are?"

"Don't make fun. I'm a conceptual poet. I teach the art of silence. I unwrite a cultural destiny that's been written and over written. I convert the stain of the visible to the pure radiance of the invisible. I repatriate the spirit from the realm of determinism to that of potential."

"I didn't mean to be sarcastic, Marty. I don't pretend to understand what you're doing. What I was getting at was if you're broke, why don't you come out here. I could get you a job writing, I'm sure you could handle it."

"You're sure I could handle it! You're sure I could handle it! Are you kidding me? The only reason I couldn't handle it is I wouldn't want to touch it."

"Now, look, Marty, there's no reason to get snotty about it. You do what you do and I do what I do and they're both valid. We're not identical twins, only fraternal, remember?"

"Listen, first of all there's no validity at all to what you're doing and I want to get that clear once and for all. And the fact we once spent nine months together in close quarters doesn't give you any authority to make judgments about what I'm doing compared to what you're doing. In fact you're not doing anything but making money, so it's not even worth talking about. You could just as well be running a hardware store."

"What's wrong with money? It's democratic. It lets people get ahead. The only thing I like more than money is power. My advice to you is to stop bitching and whining and complaining about everything and get some money and power."

"Look, when we were in college I made the decision I wanted to be a real artist. Now I am. One day you look back and realize it's your whole life and that's that. You know Rod, we're at an age when we start thinking about death. I need to be discovered Rod. I mean I know all about posterity but these days who knows whether there'll even be a posterity, some schmuck terrorist with an A-bomb in a basement could blow posterity into oblivion because he sneezed at the wrong moment, or for love of God, or because his girl friend was mean to him. You're in touch with the big machine, come on baby."

"The people I'm in touch with have no idea of the value of your work."

"The people who make reputations don't have any idea of the value of anybody's work. Come on, brother, don't let me down."

"I'll do whatever I can do but don't expect much. You have to realize that in my position you live in a completely empty world. It's just a succession of cheap thrills and in the end you're left with nothing. Your prestige, your seductions, your trips to Paris, the very house you're sitting in and the clouds in the sky, all fake, and all you have is your ability to fake it and like what's the point and you know you're in big trouble. At least you, you're doing something genuine, something in the end we can all look to and say that's what it's all about."

"Sure. You can sit there next to your jacuzzi telling me I know what it's all about. Well I can tell you what it's all about is sitting there next to your jacuzzi."

"We've made our choices."

"Why can't we have both?"

"Why not? Why can't we have everything?"

"Why can't we," sings Marty.

"Have everything," sings Drackenstein.

"Why can't we have everything," they chorus.

"Well. Seeya buddy," says Marty.

"Yeah. Keep punching," says Drackenstein. He hangs up and dials Claire's number.

"Hello?"

"How is she?"

"She's got herpes."

"Oh shit."

"She wants to get in the movies."

"All of a sudden?"

"She's decided Vegas is not where it's at, as she puts it."

"Well that's something. What was she doing there for christ sake? Tricking?"

"Don't know. Not anymore anyway. Not with herpes."

"Well that's something."

"Yes. So is herpes."

"Asher got her out?"

"On bond."

"What kind of shape's she in?"

"Sometimes hysterical sometimes depressed."

"Oh shit."

"She's got something with drugs."

"A habit?"

"Don't know."

"Poor kid. It's a hassle for you."

"Yes, it's a hassle. But at least something's happening. I mean it's company."

"I thought you liked being alone."

"Given the company available."

"I know what you mean." He wanted to hug her.

"You have no idea what I mean."

"Do you hear from Richard?"

"No."

"How come? It's over?"

"It was over before it began."

"What are you doing with yourself."

"Watching TV."

"You hate TV."

"Yes."

"You wouldn't believe it if I told you I loved you."

"No"

"Well I'll call."

"Don't call too late. I go to bed early."

"Right. Goodbye."

"Right. Goodbye."

By the time Drackenstein gets done with the calls it will be late afternoon. Plotz will have been due almost an hour ago for a conference, he wonders what's happened to him. Much later he'll remember how, in another place in the story, Crab calls him up to tell him Plotz is dead.

"How do you know?" says Drackenstein.

"I just know. He killed himself. Overdosed on sleeping pills, just like that. As if he were taking aspirin for a headache."

Drackenstein calls Victor's number but doesn't get an answer, then goes out for a paper to look for an obituary. It's Sunday. He has to put a lot of coins in the slot then spends a lot of time paging through sections of the Sunday *Times*. Finally there it is. He was fifty-two. Divorced. No kids.

Driving back to the Drackenschloss he notices something black at the side of the road. He stops. Walks back. Black. White paws. Long fur. He lifts him a little with the point of his toe to show the white chest. The only Nepalese-style Persian in the neighborhood.

He calls Plotz but there's no answer. He goes up on the deck, and spots the great beast, his unmistakable long black and white coat lit up by a shaft of sunlight, coming across the patio meowing for his food. He opens a can for him then comes back to the patio and looks out over the ravine, the rows of cypress, the steep bushy hills rolling away into the blond distance where you can hear the coyotes howl at night. It's a clear day for once, just a light haze. The soft golden light of California is like nothing else he's ever seen, he thinks, unlike the hard clear light of the Rockies and the Southwest, totally different from the pale, thin light of the east. When people from the east come out to live in that radiance you can see them change after a while, relax, open out, soften up. They ripen. Their eyes get wider, their voices deeper, their speech slows. One woman told him her breasts got larger. She also said her head got smaller. Just then he sees Plotz driving up. Plotz is one person who hasn't changed, he's too New York to ever change. Drackenstein goes downstairs to meet him. "You look like something out of one of your horror movies," he tells Drackenstein. A good New York line, thinks Drackenstein.

"I feel like somebody put me together out of old body parts today," Drackenstein says. "By the way I read the beginning of your prenovelization. How come you start with the main character committing suicide?"

"I'm writing it in order of importance, and it seems to me the most important thing that happens to anyone is death."

"Then how come he's alive again in the next chapter?"

"Because," Plotz says, "the book consists of his memory of what happens as it unreels in his mind in a flash while he's drowning."

"Miracle isn't going to like it Victor. It's already too complicated. It's too complicated from the beginning."

"By the way," says Plotz, "I use that incident where we were running out of money during the *Pig* production in the prenovelization."

"You mean with that guy Elmer Perkin? Nippy's father, the millionaire?"

"Right," says Plotz, "except in the prenovelization he's Fletcher the Letcher and Clover is Mandy. I figure the more we use things that really happened to her the easier it will be for her to play the Mandy role when we get the final script."

"I feel sort of guilty about that episode now," says Drackenstein.

"Yeah, but on the other hand if you didn't pull it off *Pig* wouldn't have got made and neither would Clover. Let me read it to you."

Plotz opens the manuscript with a certain amount of flourish.

At heart he's always wanted to be a novelist, he actually published a novel in his youth, and his hero is Henry Miller with whom he plays ping-pong now and then at Miller's place in Pacific Palisades.

"This episode of the prenovelization takes place after they've left the island and Propper is manipulating Mandy's career. They're trying to talk her into going down to 'beautiful Balboa Bay, Mandy, to spend the night on a yacht, that's real class sweetheart,' urged Propper, 'I'm not asking you to turn a trick for christ sake, it's a question of whether Fletcher Bennington is going to put up the rest of the bread for the film, because if we can't finish the film we'll all be fucked and that's that.'

"'You're asking me to sell my pussy is what I'm hearing.' Mandy was sulking. Actually Propper knew Mandy could, under some circumstances, get a kick out of selling her pussy and that was what he was counting on. It had to be safe, it had to be classy with a lot of money involved, there had to be a reasonable possibility she could get into it with the particular guy, in other words it had to be something like a date combined with a fantasy trip.

"'I'm not asking you to sell anything. You know I'm only interested in your welfare. You might like the guy. Who knows you might fall in love and get married. All I'm asking you to do is go down to Newport and have a little fun, I don't think that's so much to ask.' Actually Bennington was a star screwer. He was known as Fletcher the Letcher. The yacht, called *Marilyn*, had never been seen unmoored from its dock.

"Propper drove her down to Newport. She was on speed and very wired. Bennington's big yacht docked in Balboa Bay would have been even more impressive had it not been dwarfed by John Wayne's converted destroyer moored nearby. Bennington waved to them from the bow where he was talking with a greying gent in a yachting cap who looked a lot like him. They both had their hands in their blazer pockets and were looking out across the harbor as if they owned it. A gorgeous, dark-haired and very well dressed young woman was standing some distance from them near the cabin. Mandy and Propper went on board. Bennington came and introduced them to Sara, then excused himself and went back to his friend, saying he had some business to finish up. Propper left them there, the two old gents, smug and complicitous, the two girls waiting behind them with an air of mutual comprehension. When he picked her up the next morning her face was tight, pale, fatigued, she looked like death, he never asked her what happened. By the way, what happened?" Plotz asks.

"I don't know, I never asked," says Drackenstein.

Drackenstein will decide to take Clover down to Marineland for an afternoon to get her away from it all. On the way down he'll show her a gossip column clipping Miracle will have sent to him.

STAR LIKES BOSS. We bumped into Clover Bottom and her formidable upper structure in the spumoni colored lobby of the Beverly Hills Hotel Friday and, ogled by all and sundry, followed her mon dieu derriere into the Polo Lounge for drinks. Clover has, among other things, the roundest fanny on the silver screen, for the information of fanny fans. The romantic link between Clover and Rod Drackenstein is no secret among insiders. He recently gifted her with a new yellow Stingray so she doesn't have to hitchhike anymore.

"The impressive thing about Rod is how hard he works,"

she confided. "His intensity is amazing. He makes great demands on his actors and on himself, but when a shooting script is finally set he stops worrying and just goes ahead and has fun. That's the secret of how he can make his films so economically."

Asked about Drackenstein's reputation for exploiting women, Clover bristled. "That's just gossip," she said. "No one is kinder or more considerate, or so much fun to work with. Sometimes the pressures are so great I worry he's going to have a breakdown, but he never forgets to be polite. Rod is actually very sensitive. His image as a heavy is for the public. In a way it's good publicity for the kind of pictures he makes, and he even likes to encourage it. It's a role."

You mean like John Simon? we asked.

"Yes," she said, sipping her gin and tonic thoughtfully. "Actually Rod has a lot of integrity. And contrary to his media reputation, in private he is actually a feminist. The best way to put it, I guess, is that Rod is human."

Clover Bottom is starring in a new Drackenstein film called *Blown Away*, soon to be lensed.

When Clover gets done reading this she says, "Who's John Simon? I don't remember any of this."

"Of course you don't," says Drackenstein. "I gave the interview for you over the phone."

Instead of taking the freeway directly to Marineland, Drackenstein detours into the hills of Palos Verdes, above the coast. He'll turn off to the Wayfarer's Chapel, Lloyd Wright's little church of glass, where he sometimes goes to get it together, not out of anything you would think of as religious motivation, but because it brings together the past and the present for him. He'll remember how he used to drop off at the chapel when he was a kid, on the way to the beach. In those days Palos Verdes is a wilderness, just a few big estates going down to the cliffs and beaches. He knows this kid whose parents own one. They go swimming on completely deserted beaches, explore sea caves tunneling through Portuguese Point that maybe only a few people have ever seen besides them. Once they meet W.C. Fields walking down the beach with a woman and a thermos of martinis. Los Angeles in the old days, before the tracts and the freeways. Orange groves everywhere. Mountains visible somewhere in the distance with snow on them. There's a trolley all the way down to Balboa where you can take the ferry to the Fun Zone. If you want to go out to the Valley you have to go up Cahuenga Boulevard. The Arroyo Seco in Pasadena must be the greatest place ever to play touch football. At night there are always search lights needling the sky, whether for a new drugstore or car lot or a film opening. Madman Muntz is selling cars and Wolfman Jack selling music. The world premieres are ceremonies of hope. Little Roddie would go watch the stars get out of their limousines and walk in on red carpets, flash bulbs popping like fire crackers. When he was little he used to try to fit his feet into the footprints at Grauman's. For years he thinks Charlie McCarthy is real. Maybe it all collapsed, Drackenstein speculates, when Chaplin left. After that Mickey Mouse became a sinister figure, a name for what was cheap and unreal. Or is it the same as ever, he thinks, and me who's become cheap and unreal? They go into the Chapel. Its glass admits sheets of radiance that dissolve the barrier between interior and exterior space, and looking at a wall, you see not a painting of the world as in other churches, but the world itself of which the Chapel, through its transparency, declares itself part.

"The trouble with me," he tells Clover, "is that I never find myself doing anything that's not basically for myself these days. Back in the sixties commitment meant more than dedication to your career."

I remember how, later, Drackenstein will tell Plotz that if for the middle class life is unreal, for the poor it's too real.

"And what's real for you," Plotz asks.

"Power, money, charm, the usual bullshit," Drackenstein will tell him.

Clover is looking into her pocket mirror and arranging her hair, a gesture that annoys Drackenstein for some reason. "Really," she says.

"You know what happened to Narcissus, he drowned."

"What are you saying Rod?"

"How can you stand there looking in your mirror in the middle of a beautiful gem like this?"

"What's wrong with you? Since I'm always on display I have to look good, and I guess this is the original glass house. Are you getting jealous?" She puts the mirror away. It reminds me how, way off toward the end, she'll get up in the morning, shower and examine herself nude in the mirror, as every morning, slowly rubbing cream into her belly skin, her thighs, her buttocks, her breasts, squeezing the nipples a little between thumbs and index fingers till they come erect. She likes to look at herself, she likes to be looked at. She's fascinated with her own image. Every morning this way she reenters the land of enchantment, entranced by the mirror. Hypnotized, she moves through the house to the door opening into the garage, gets topless into the

Stingray, starts motor as garage door slides up, the rest is headlines.

"I'm not jealous," says Drackenstein, "I'm just trying to figure out the best way to stay afloat these days."

As soon as they get into Marineland people will start noticing Clover. It's not only that she's spectacular. The centerfold spread is out and the famous nude poster is plastered all over the city, the hottest item in every head shop and greeting card outlet in the country, Clover on the bed with her ass up in the air, done in imitation, as the photographer loves to point out, of Boucher's "Mrs. O'Murphy." And there's a slightly more discreet but colossal version on a Sunset Boulevard billboard. Like some exotic animal, Clover is on display wherever she goes. Soon there's a group trailing them, pointing and murmuring.

In the whale arena they go down close to the glass panel enclosing the tank, trying to avoid the first occasional autograph hunters coming up to Clover. Soon though there are so many they can hardly pay attention to the show as the whales are let into the pool. Drackenstein hands Clover the various postcards, programs, and envelopes that they pass to him. The killer whales are leaping into the air, tons of them, coming down with enormous splashes. Jumping for bait suspended way up above the pool.

"They're so beautiful. Why do they make them do that?" asks Clover, signing somebody's blank check and passing it back to Drackenstein.

"Show biz," he says. "That's how they make a living."

They're getting wet from the splashing. Drackenstein turns around and tries to pull Clover back away from the tank but discovers they're surrounded by a dense ring of people.

"Is that Clover Bottom?" says a kid.

"You want to make way please," Drackenstein says. "Can we get through?"

The M.C. interrupts his P.A. patter. "I would like to welcome beautiful Clover Bottom to Marineland today," the P.A. booms. "And so would Corky."

They're getting soaked. The whole crowd is getting soaked but it won't move. It starts to press in, people start reaching out to touch Clover.

"Is that really Clover Bottom?"

"I want to touch her."

"I want to hold her hand."

"I want to grab her ass."

"Get away, beat it," Drackenstein yells. He can see Clover is starting to panic. An avalanche of water falls on them as Corky splashes down just on the other side of the barrier. People scatter. Drackenstein grabs Clover's arm and they make a break up the arena stairs. The crowd regroups and starts after them. Drackenstein can't believe this is happening. A couple of guards trying to run interference are quickly swept aside but give them just enough time to reach an exit which is slammed shut behind them.

They get back to the Stingray, Clover soaked and sobbing.

"I thought we were going to have to jump into the tank," she gasps.

"And get gulped by the whale? Not me."

Drackenstein will be staring at the license plates covering the ceiling of Barney's Beanery when Plotz walks in.

"What are we doing here?" asks Plotz.

"We're waiting for Wang. We have an old habit of meeting here. He says it's the only place he can get Tahitian beer."

"You know how I first came to this place?" asks Plotz. "I went over to the County Museum to see Kienholz's replica, 'Barney's Beanery' and when I asked a guard where it was, he goes, 'Oh that's somewhere over around La Cienega.' Turned out the show was gone anyway so I came over here. Figured if I wasn't going to see 'Barney's Beanery' I could at least get to see Barney's Beanery. So what do you think?"

"It's good. I love it. It suggests her hooker side and gives us a little space for some sexy scenes later on. Only five will have to go."

"What's wrong with five?"

"It's talky and digressive. It doesn't stick with the plot we've laid out. Besides all that talk about reality and unreality is unreal. For the middle class life is unreal, for the poor it's too real, that's all it amounts to. The poor and the rich are in touch with the powers that shape their lives, but the middle class lives in a manipulated revery. I should know, I'm one of the manipulators."

"And what's real for you, Rod?"

"Nothing. It's all bullshit. Power, money, charm, you know the scene as well as I do. There's nothing there. You'd have to change your life to find something real in the Fuck You Generation." God, I'm starting to sound like Crab, Drackenstein thinks. He's going to sound a lot more like Crab as Crab moves in and takes possession. I'm Ccrab.

One evening Crab is at the Drackenschloss visiting Clover. Drackenstein goes to sleep early. Clover herself is nodding in front of the fire looking exhausted. There's something dead about her, Crab thinks. He has the feeling he's trying to bring her back to life. He's thinking that maybe if he could reestablish their sexual relations, that if he could make her come, he might make her come back, and anyway, it's hard not coming on to her again so why fight it. Thinking about it makes him feel spaced out, a little faint. He gets up and goes to the john, and when he looks in the mirror he's not surprised to find it empty. When he comes back he finds Crab sitting in his chair, looking very faint. Crab sits down next to him. "How do you feel?" Crab asks him.

"Very faint," says Crab.

"So do I," says Crab. "I have to go to the john. He who sees his going double himself must go."

Crab doesn't give a second thought to hallucinations. It seems to him he's living in a hallucination. A hallucination he's still trying to control, partly through his influence on Clover, partly through Crab's metamorphic influence on Drackenstein. Even Plotz is becoming more sympathetic in the general flux, the hidden sensitivity indicated by the delicate fuchsia band in his aura becoming more pronounced. And who knows what might happen even to Miracle caught among the occult crosscurrents of experience? But it's fatiguing. We are definitely overextended. I myself have given up the fortune to become the teller. It is written, as they say. Clover is acting out her part, her submissiveness to Drackenstein, the way he can make her come when called, the way he can make her come, is all part of her death trip. Though even when Drackenstein tells her to come now she's late, she comes, but she comes later and later, she's always late for everything, throws schedules off, screws up promo dates, begins to cost Drackenstein money and when something costs Drackenstein money he gets furious, but it doesn't do any good, she comes, but she comes late. And sometimes depressed or incoherent from drugs. Also she's gaining weight and it's starting to affect her figure, her face is getting real porky, she's hardly eating anything but she gains weight anyway. Finally Drackenstein puts her on a fast every third day, it helps but it really spaces her out the days she isn't eating, she gets through them on speed. It's around then they start supplying her with coke, it's good for the diet. Drackenstein is already whispering about getting a stand-in for Clover.

One day Crab, feeling romantic, meets Clover at the Santa Monica pier, and they'll stroll over to the old building that houses the carrousel. Clover says she wants to listen to the merry-go-round music. She says it makes her sad.

"How come you want to be sad?" Crab asks.

"I've been getting friendly with Madame Lazonga," she says, she still calls Clara Madame Lazonga, "and Madame Lazonga says I should be more in touch with my feelings. Madame Lazonga says I have a lot of sad feelings, and maybe listening to the merry-go-round music is a good way of getting in touch with them. Plus Madame Lazonga told me I ought to stay away from men. Madame Lazonga says that men are exploiting me by draining my vital essence. I don't understand what vital essence is but whatever, I'm all fucked out. Truly. So I'm not into screwing with you anymore. Please don't take it personally Boris. I'm not screwing with anybody else anymore either. I'm tired of people trying to fuck me."

At this point Crab actually starts wondering about using Wang's love potion. "Is it because you don't have orgasms with me anymore?" he asks.

"I don't care about orgasms. I've had plenty of orgasms with other men. I've had all the orgasms I want. What I want is to preserve my vital essence because I'm feeling all fucked out. If I want to have orgasms I can use my vibrator. Or jerk off, I don't need men. Madame Lazonga says that sex is a violation of privacy. She says women need to be independent."

"Does all that apply to Drackenstein?"

"Rod's different," says Clover. "Rod is part of my real life. My real life is the movies, I am supposed to be a sex goddess after all."

Then they'll have their first real fight since the Sargon incident. Crab walks out angry, and Clover, dabbing at her eyes with a Kleenex, buys a ride on the carrousel, in a chariot going around and around as the music plays feeling, for reasons she can't pin down, sorry for herself. She decides to go shopping in Beverly Hills.

A few days later, though, inevitably, Crab will take Clover up to the mountains around Elsinore for a therapy weekend with Dr. Roxoff, hoping she'll get it together. She's in such bad shape that Drackenstein has to okay her absence even though it means money. If she can't get through the filming it's going to cost much more. Crab drives her up there and waits for her in Elsinore, a gambling town where there's nothing to do but wallow around in a shallow lake, eat in an Italian restaurant and play cards. It seems to be a popular resort spot. Parachuting seems to be the big local sport in Elsinore, there are always several bright parachutes hanging in the air. Crab finds them comforting, lying on the beach and falling asleep watching the parachutes floating down. He begins thinking of the place as El Snore.

Sunday evening Crab picks Clover up at the therapy center. Clover doesn't say a word but she looks good, her face looks relaxed, her voice is deeper, her aura has a healthy glow to it for the first time in months.

"So how was it?" he asks after a while.

"I learned how to hug people," Clover says.

"That's it?"

"I learned how to stand on my feet. I learned not to lean on other people. And how to get angry. Really. I feel wonderful. Even Dr. Roxoff says I feel wonderful. I haven't had any coke all weekend."

Crab drives her new Stingray down the Ortega Highway through the hills back to the coast and they stop for a taco in Capistrano. Clover tells him all about herself. She's too dependent. She relates to men as father figures. She's a perennial daughter. She needs sisterhood. She's okay. Crab isn't okay. He's always trying to be her father. She doesn't need another father, Crab is trying to exploit her.

"Plus Dr. Roxoff says I'm angry at you. You bastard. You can go fuck yourself. The same goes for Rod."

"Sounds like a very effective weekend. But it's getting late so let's go."

"Don't say let's go to me," she says. "I'll drive."

She peels out of the parking lot accelerating fast. "Slow down," Crab tells her, "put your lights on," she doesn't answer she puts the lights on. She slams a cassette into the deck mouth and turns it up so loud they can't talk. By the time they hit the freeway she's already doing seventy Crab yelling at her to slow down when he sees the DO NOT ENTER sign flash past.

"Hey you're going the wrong way my god Clover stop the car," but they're already on the freeway going about eighty miles an hour the wrong way a set of headlights zips past another ahead is flicking and yawing Crab screaming reaching over and jams his hand against the horn she veers to the side of the road hits the brake the car swinging out of control slides sideways to a stop the music throbbing. Crab is slapping at her she has her hands over her eyes, screaming, "I'm sorry I'm sorry it was a mistake."

"You were trying to kill us," he yells, turning off the music.

"All right all right all right all right," she's sobbing.

He gets her out of the car and changes places with her, turns the car around and drives very slowly to the next exit.

"I wonder what Roxoff would say about that," says Crab.

The week after they get back Clover will start studying T'ai Chi with Dong Wang. Drackenstein doesn't like the idea but Clover is so shaky he doesn't dare interfere. "I think what she's really studying is Dong's Wang," he says to Plotz. But he's wrong. Wang is horny but not that horny.

"She's so dead at this point it would be like fucking a corpse," he tells Crab. "What I'm doing with her is teaching her the concept of 'my space.'" My space is something that nobody can come into without her permission. It begins to appear that despite Drackenstein's suspicions that she's screwing Wang, and even Crab, nobody has her permission to come into my space anymore except maybe Nippy Perkin. She and Nippy go up to Malibu for a few days together while Plotz and Drackenstein are trying to polish the shooting script. Every once in a while you see them holding hands in quiet corners of U.Ip. Finally Clover comes and tells Crab, who has become her confidante, that she's really heavy into Nippy, as if asking Crab what he thinks about it. "I know it," is all Crab says. The trouble is it has nothing to do with Drackenstein. It's a desperation move on Clover's part to fight free of the power men exercise over her. But ironically the affair begins in the course of a long conversation she and Nippy have about the time Clover went down to Newport to screw her father on his yacht. It turns out that Elmer Perkin also exercises a certain erotic power over his daughter, just as Drackenstein does over Clover. He still has that power over her but he's willing to let Clover go off on whatever sex trip for the time being as long as it helps hold her together for the movie.

Drackenstein will feel extremely divided. He feels guilty about trying to manipulate Clover and jealous about her sexual adventures. But he also feels he's holding her fragile ego to-gether, along with the whole project, through sheer force of will. The intensity of his self-hatred recently is the measure of this ambivalence. Clover is more than a lover to him by now, she's almost like a daughter. He'll remember how she's barely a grownup at the beginning of the story, knowing but inarticulate, ignorant, unevolved, how the first time he goes to visit her in her apartment she offers him some "vin" and he has to tell her "that rhymes with tan, Cathy June, not skin." How she grows to identify with the way she looks in her many images till the way she is is the way she looks. How he notices even then that her favorite occupation seems to be looking at herself in the mirror, so that even when she undresses for the first time she's looking not at him but at her reflection, so that even in his first view of her there are two of her. And how when he asks her to do things as they make love she answers, "Do I have to?" like a thirteen year old, as if she needs to be forced, that streak of inturned violence her answer to pervasive sexual aggression, till later he'll understand that her submissiveness is not passive but passionate, an exercise of power however inverted. Thinking he's entrancing her with his charm, his magnetism, he suddenly realizes one day she's already in a trance, never awakened to a normal level of consciousness, numbed by simplicity, stunned with easy pleasure, stunted education, blank look on face at words of more than two syllables, "What does criterion mean?" She acts the same way around Crab, whom she allows to believe he can hypnotize her, his own control obsessions dividing and subdividing in paranoid hallucinations, as if she wants to be hypnotized. Or you might say he does hypnotize her, in any case through his influence instilling a kind of consciousness in those blank blue eyes, a consciousness nevertheless inadequate to her situation.

On top of everything else, Drackenstein is quarreling with Plotz about the script. The production is behind schedule, the plot still isn't shaping up. What Drackenstein doesn't know is that Plotz is mostly at work on the renovelization not the prenovelization, writing furiously all night night after night, getting almost no sleep, inspired by an encounter with Henry Miller. He attends a lecture at U.C.L.A. by Miller and afterwards goes to say a few words to him. Miller comes walking up the aisle with Durrell, who happens to be in town, fending off the crowd. Miller shakes Plotz's hand, looks him in the eye and says, "Keep punching." Then Durrell shoves Plotz away. Suddenly Plotz knows what he has to do is write the whole story of the film, what really happens, the truth, not the insipid *Tempest* ripoff. In fact the hell with the film. Plotz knows this is his last chance and he's engaged in a frantic life or death gamble, letting everything else go to hell.

And everything is going to hell. That day Clover is late. She's having a big fight with Nippy, and gets to the set red eyed and hysterical. Crab manages to calm her down some. But when Nippy walks onto the set Clover blows it. "I want you to fire that cunt," she screams. "I'm not working while she's on this film." "Look," says Drackenstein, "I know you're learning to express aggression sweetheart," he starts yelling, "but this is costing me money and I have no intention of paying for your hangups," he calms down, "so let's push on, shall we? Take a break, I want to talk to Victor."

He waves the unfinished manuscript of the prenovelization at

Plotz. "Victor, what are we supposed to do with this bit in here about Mandy getting pregnant? First of all, she's supposed to have been isolated on an island in the company of no one but her father, her brother and a faggot. I think you'll have to agree this raises more problems than it solves. On top of that can you envision a snuff scene with a pregnant woman?

"No," says Plotz. "That's the point."

"Look," says Drackenstein, "I want you to go up to Lompoc this weekend and make absolutely god damn sure you work it in. Miracle wants it in, so you can make it arty but get it in. We'll do the industry's first quality snuff sequence."

"We don't have a location planned for it."

"Okay then find a location."

"Sure, Rod." Actually what Plotz is planning to do in Lompoc is to try to finish a draft of the renovelization with which he's totally obsessed, he's in a trance, he can't think about anything else. It's like some kind of ongoing seizure.

That weekend Crab will go to see Clover, she's still waking up, one in the afternoon, eating breakfast, yogurt and granola with a glass of Southern Comfort on the rocks, Jimi Hendrix destroying his guitar on the stereo. She's losing too much weight and is starting to look pallid. Driving up to the house Crab expects to see Nippy somewhere in this scene but by the time he gets there he knows she isn't going to be. Clover tells him she isn't into Nippy anymore.

"I'm not into anybody right now," she says. "I don't see why I have to be fucking somebody all the time." She says she's into a thing, what Madame Lazonga calls The New Chastity. She says Madame Lazonga says that sex is becoming vulgar and evasive, common, consumer oriented, that it's counter-revolutionary, that it's no longer distinguished. She says Madame Lazonga says the only way out is to get into The New Chastity.

"I'm into masturbation," says Clover. "I've never been into masturbation because as soon as I was old enough to get into masturbation I got into fucking. When I was a kid masturbation was a nono you weren't supposed to masturbate you were supposed to fuck. I was just conforming." She says she's really getting into being a vegetarian she isn't even eating eggs anymore. She finishes off her bowl of yogurt and granola and washes it down with the rest of the Southern Comfort and a cup of Pero. And a pill. There are bottles of pills scattered all over the table. A typical California diet, drugs and health food.

"Plus I'm thinking of getting rolfed, I heard about this neat woman in San Diego." She wants to know what Crab thinks about reincarnation, she says Wang is getting her interested in Buddhism, she's thinking of flying out to Boulder to see somebody called Rinpoche Trungpa from Tibet, she's wearing a Buddhist red string necklace, she says she's trying to read the *Tibetan Book of the Dead* but it's hard to get into.

"I've always had a thing about life after death," she says. "I still sort of believe in some kind of heaven. That's why I've never been afraid of dying, which is strange because I'm afraid of almost everything else."

As I recall it will be shortly after that when Crab goes up to Drackenstein's place in the hills hoping to catch him without an appointment and talk to him about Clover. He knows something is wrong, a feeling of doom, then suddenly he knows what it is. Drackenstein is there, but in a terrible mood.

"Plotz is dead again," says Crab. "This time it's for real."

"He wiped out on the Grapevine," says Drackenstein. "Sideswiped by a semi."

"I know."

"What was he doing on the Grapevine? I thought he was going to Lompoc."

"He did," Crab explains to Drackenstein. "But he decided to go up north to look at the Winchester Mystery House and the Madonna Inn as possible locations to use in the snuff sequence, then he came back on 5 through Paso Robles and over the mountains where, exhausted by his marathon renovelization effort, he fell asleep at the wheel."

"I called his ex-wife to tell her. You know what she said? She said, 'Tough shit,' and hung up."

"Poor Victor," says Crab.

"Yeah. Poor Victor. But I'll tell you one thing, he sure left me holding the bag. The script is a complete fuck up. What's the Madonna Inn?"

"You know, that kind of poor man's Hearst Castle where everything is not only imitation but imitation of various pop imitations, like the 'Daisy Mae Bathroom.'"

"And of course he was after the gothic touch in the Winchester House. Mazes, rooms within rooms, stairways leading nowhere. Which is a lot like his crazy plots, come to think of it. Is that what he had in mind?" Drackenstein shakes a manuscript at Crab. "Or was he giving up in despair?"

"Is that all you can think of at this moment?"

"That's what I have to think of. It's like there's a curse on this film." Drackenstein looks at Crab suspiciously.

"What do you want from me," says Crab.

"Take a look," says Drackenstein, shoving the manuscript at him. "They found it in the car, it's a mess."

The cover sheet says, "BLOWN AWAY, a California novel, by Victor Plotz," and below that, "To the Unhappy Few," and below that what seems to be a smudge of blood like a brushy signature in a Japanese painting.

"It seems that Victor was already at work on renovelization, in fact he came fairly close to finishing. It turns out to be not the story in the film, but a story about the production of the film, including intimate scandal portraits of everyone involved."

"Everyone?" asks Crab.

"You, me, everyone. Including Plotz himself. I don't know what the fuck he thought he was doing. But any ideas in there we can use to finish the film are going to be used. And if it's any good at all I'm going to have the lawyers look it over and publish the damn thing, maybe we can make a buck on it. I want you to look it over. It's confused toward the end where he didn't have time to finish, lists, notes, contradictions, disconnected scenes, sketches for scenes and a long revision. But that's no problem we can always hire a ghost. Get some cockamamie avant garde writer and push it as experimental fiction. But experimental fiction that everybody can understand. Why should the masses be deprived of elite art?"

Crab goes off into another room to look at the thing: According to Plotz, they have Clover going down to Fletcher Bennington's yacht in Newport Beach to raise money for the *Blown Away* project before Miracle gets into the act. Fletcher Bennington is obviously a thinly disguised portrait of Elmer Perkin, instantly recognizable to anyone who knows anything at all. Why Plotz bothered to disguise Perkin, especially when he doesn't extend the same dubious courtesy to the rest of us, is a mystery, thinks Crab, unless he was afraid his ektachromatic descriptions of Bennington's weird sex habits would be inhibited by the threat of Perkin suing him. Anything in order to tell the truth, even not telling the truth. Or is it because Perkin is Downtown—San Marino, Golf and Poker Club, Community

Committee. "I'm not asking you to turn a trick or anything for christ sake," Drackenstein tells her.

"You're asking me to sell my pussy is what I'm hearing."

"Okay put it this way. A fuck is just a pole up the hole, but if we can't raise the bread to finish the film we'll all be fucked."

A tear appears on Clover's cheek. Drackenstein softens but not much. He knows Clover is one of the few actresses who can cry at will. It's one of her few talents. "Look," he says, "who knows, you might like the guy. You might fall in love and get married. All I'm asking you to do is go down to Newport and have a little fun, I don't think that's so much to ask."

Finally they convince Clover to go down to visit Bennington on his yacht, and what happens is Miracle is there on the boat with another girl and really falls for Clover. And that's how Miracle gets involved with the production. Clover has a great time and when she comes back and tells Drackenstein he gets jealous as hell.

But as soon as Miracle gets involved the film goes from bad to horrible, according to Plotz. And so does Clover who, already extremely shaky from being in a scene she hasn't the resources to handle, is by now constantly on the edge. Crab isn't much better off. His energies are definitely at the point of running out.


Goes to see Lazonga.

More and more insubstantial.

Sun makes real.

Mickey mouse. Mickey mouse no soul. Mickey Mouse right.

e ie e.

Bad dreams.

In the Plotz manuscript I, that is, Crab, decide to go down to Venice and visit Lazonga. Lazonga gives him a pep talk. She says it isn't Crab's life they're stealing but Clover's, and since Clover's life is really in the movies it doesn't matter anyway.

"It's true there's a correlation," says Crab. "She's becoming more and more insubstantial personally the more she gets into her public identity but you know, Clara, everybody is beginning to seem less real to me, the very idea of personality is becoming totally unconvincing beyond a minimal definition as an intersection of genes and circumstance. In fact everything's becoming unreal, I'm even beginning to seem unreal to myself."

"Go out into the sunshine, the sun makes everything real."

"That's the basic premise of California and I don't believe it. Spiritually it's strictly mickey mouse. It keeps everything at the moral level of a Walt Disney animation. I feel like I'm becoming an animation, some kind of spiritual pod. The trouble with Clover is she was never anything more than a cartoon, she's always thought of herself as a cartoon, and now she's starting to realize it's possible not to be a cartoon it's too much for her to handle."

"Mickey Mouse had the right idea," says Lazonga. "You know very well we're all living in a world of images to begin with. So stop whining and start using your imagination. And don't knock Mickey Mouse."

Here Plotz's renovelization includes a series of notes, then continues with the narrative:

Tom Hayden campaign
into seascapes
dogshit auto breakdowns razor cuts
labyrinthine halls complicated apartments empty rooms
fuck not pole up hole

"Guess what Boris. Either yours or Rod's. Throw me into the La Brea Tar Pits."

OO ICU 2 CAN DO OIAMAQT I M EZ

"Your mom is a very neat chick I really get off on her."

TOPLESS BOTTOM WREAKS HAVOC

Harley True a teamster

"That's where integrity gets you."

"Does giving head imply losing face?"

"What am I your scumbag?"

frenzy rage nymphomania depression

"Your silver cat glow. Your sad beautiful lady."

"Try to get your real feelings into it."

"Bring me back a ham sandwich."

e ie e

Clover figures if she just holds out long enough to get to the top of the heap she can tell them all to go to hell. "It's the last cock I'm going to suck," she could hear herself telling Miracle. She heard Marilyn Monroe told that to someone somewhere. But anyway she knows she's going to have to learn more, do more, if she's going to keep it together. That's what Madame Lazonga tells her and she can relate to that. That why she's into self-realization. She wants to be able to read her own mind, to have something to say about her own fortunes. I can't depend on my hypnotic sexual power to control men's minds forever, she thinks, even if they are mostly pricks. Still you get fond of people once you start making love with them, even Miracle turns out to be a kind of neat dude once you get to understand him. A fuck is not just a pole up the hole.

"Of course she's quite different now," Drackenstein tells Plotz.

"That's right," says Plotz. "She's no longer the raw kid she was when we first started working with her. She certainly was a sexy little animal though."

"But mickey mouse. Very mickey mouse. She's grown. She's developed. She's getting ideas about things. Do you know she's gotten interested in the Tom Hayden campaign?"

"She's interested in politics?" says Plotz.

"That's right. I've got her involved with some of my lefty connections. You should have heard her get on Miracle the other night about studio exploitation of women. She's going to do a benefit with Jane Fonda next week."

"No kidding."

"No kidding. And art. She's buying paintings. She's been going around to the galleries on La Cienega. She's into seascapes. I was trying to convince her to go to this hip little gallery I know up in the Hills, but she says she hears Laguna is the place for seascapes. So I drive her down to Laguna Beach and we look at about a thousand seascapes. After around five hours of shopping through the galleries she finally buys nine seascapes at seven hundred dollars apiece plus a bust of Marilyn Monroe at a place called Clyde Zulch Originals in Corona del Mar. Then she wants me to drive her back before we have a chance to eat dinner so she can go to a poetry reading. A poetry reading. How do you like them apples? So I drive her to Venice where we listen to a poetry reading for two hours at a store called Beyond Baroque and I'm starving. The poet who was reading asked for her autograph."

During this period Lazonga is doing her best to influence Clover, infiltrating her personality through inhabitation, but although Clover doesn't know it yet, she's already inhabited by pregnancy. The only result of Lazonga's attempt is an increasing ambivalence and confusion in Clover. No longer quite her vapid former self, she is assaulted by feelings she doesn't yet know how to handle, is subject to sudden fits of doubt and self hatred. One day they're talking about a screening of one of the rushes at Miracle's mansion in the hills.

"It's phony," Clover suddenly blurts out.

"What do you mean phony," says Miracle.

"I'm sorry, it's my fault," she says. "Because I'm phony. A fake, a fraud. A cartoon. I'm not smart enough, not talented enough. It's hopeless, I have no future."

"Jesus, do something Rod. She's getting hysterical," says Miracle.

"All I want to be is real," says Clover.

"Boris," says Drackenstein. "Do me a favor. Take her somewhere and talk to her." Drackenstein is feeling like he's about to puke and he's thinking he can't stand this scene much longer. Like a disc jockey he knows whose whole body swings to the music he plays on the station, snapping his fingers, and all the while muttering to himself, "What shit, what dreck, obscene."

Crab himself is feeling very faint. But as the others file out of the library I, that is, he, takes Clover to a side room and calms her down with some acupressure. "When I look at my future I don't like what I see," she says. "I have future schlock." She looks panicked, then laughs. "God, did I say that? You see, I'm learning Yiddish already."

"Go to sleep now," says Crab. He can see into her mind and what he sees is terror. When he goes back through the library he finds Crab sitting in his chair looking very faint. Or is it Crab's failing eyesight? He sits down next to him. "How do you feel?" Crab asks him.

"Very faint," says Crab.

"So do I," says Crab. "It's getting to be about time for metamorphosis. I'm feeling a strong need for a quick change. Anyway why don't you take a rest," he tells Crab. He waves his hand. "Expresso digresso." Crab evaporates.

According to Plotz's renovelization, around this time Crab manages to lay a curse on Drackenstein, but can't really get his heart into it. It turns out to be trivial, things like stepping in dog shit, auto breakdowns, razor cuts, minor business aggravations, parking tickets, piles, bad nerves. It's really Crab, not Crab, who's working on Drackenstein, doubletime, by imposing a kind of psychic osmosis on him that has an essentially humanizing effect, a process that can only result in the failure, fall, and withdrawal of Drackenstein and the annihilation of Crab by absorption into Drackenstein's personality.

Everyone is very strung out at this point, ODed on the film, except maybe Miracle. Plotz is around, according to Plotz's manuscript, but seems to confine his role mostly to that of observer. You can practically see him taking mental notes. Crab notes that Plotz, whose aura usually shades to a kind of delicate fuchsia, which possibly explains why Crab likes him despite their frequent arguments, no longer has any aura at all, a state of affairs which usually means death in life.

I myself can't help but note that Plotz's manuscript really cuts to the chase at this point in the action. It's as if Plotz finally has given up trying to make his fortune on the story and is just telling it without thinking about it, letting it flow through him like a medium does. Maybe it requires a certain amount of stupidity to get plots moving, and Plotz is finally moving, though he had to get himself killed off to do it, that's always moving though it's a cheap trick, but neat plots are always based on cheap tricks. Plotz now aspires to be a professor of stupidity, he has no ideas, he's less informed than his characters, he has no opinion about what's going to happen next, he has no claim to

expertise other than his repertoire of tricks that work like a
magic show on the audience but are a source of despair to
himself. Is this the reason, rather than lack of time, for the hasty
and sometimes notational style here, as if by stripping the stage
bare and exposing what little artifice remains he might allow
some stain of truth to seep through? the truth, simply, of what
happens, starting with death and going on from there?

Anyway, according to Plotz, what happens, as Crab of course
already knows, is that Clover is going to discover she's pregnant.
Crab gets a call from her one night. "Guess what Boris!" she
says.

"I don't have to guess Clo," he tells her. She's laughing over
the phone.

"What's so funny?" Crab asks.

"Really," she says. "This is beautiful. I really lucked out didn't
I. Rod wants me to wait till after we finish the film. If I wait till
after the film it might be too late. I'm not into having it, plus I
don't get off on kids. Madame Lazonga's arranged the doctor
and everything. Tomorrow. Rod is really pissed."

"Do you know whose it is?"

"For sure," she says. "Mine."

When Crab goes to see her the next day she seems all right
for someone who's just had an abortion except she looks like a
zombie. She's lying in the sun on the patio wrapped in a blanket
sipping Southern Comfort on the rocks and listening to Janis
singing "Bobby McGee."

"I used to think you didn't have to pay for things," she says.
She laughs. "I should have known. My mom used to say she was
going to throw me into the La Brea Tar Pits when I was bad. It's
all fucked." Crab notices her voice is deeper, emptied of its
characteristic little girl quality.

"What can I do for you?" asks Crab.

"Nothing, I'm cool," says Clover.

Clover wants to go visit her mother she hasn't seen her in four years. Four years. Crab drives her down to Santa Ana past the Babylonian UniRoyal factory Japanese Deer Park Disney's Matterhorn Knott's Berry Farm mad king ludwig minigolf castles and license plate graffiti saying OO ICU, 2 CAN DO, OIMAQT, I M EZ into Orange County turning off the freeway near a movie theater that looks like two giant breasts into a subdivision surrounded by gala rows of tall pennants crackling in the wind. The ranch style house looks real neat from the outside but when her mother opens the door they see that inside everything's a mess. Clover's mother, Veronica, looks like a fifty year old twenty year old, and has her hair down over one eye like Veronica Lake thirty years ago.

"Oh hi honey, I hear you're doing good. This big hulk here is the dude I'm getting it on with."

A shoeless shirtless blond, muscular, of indeterminate age, gets up off the sofa, full of good humor.

"Okay! your mom is a really neat chick she's my old lady I really get off on her."

"Yeah on me and every other chick shows her face around here tell him it's not a nice way to treat your mother," her eyes suddenly going bleary.

"Now Veronica, don't get into it okay," says Clover.

"Don't worry honey I'm really mellowed out," flicking her cigarette in the wastebasket. "You want a joint or some pills them little red downs are a nice trip."

"No Veronica, we're taking a drive we have to go now."

"Okay Cathy June see you later," her mother says.

"That must have taken about four minutes," Clover says as Crab steers through the labyrinth subdivision. "That's about right, a minute every year, next time I'll save them up till I hit ten." She shoves a James Brown tape into the mouth of the cassette deck and turns it up loud. Back on the freeway heading for L.A. they're almost driven off the road by a couple of crazy surfers smoking and drinking beer in a speeding van painted with a mural of Los Angeles crumbling in an earthquake and a bumper sticker that says,"Hang On You're in Shaky City." License plates they see: 4 GOT  YEN 4 ME.

At the same time Crab is down in Santa Ana with Clover he's also walking along Hollywood Boulevard with Drackenstein. "Where's she at Professor?" asks Drackenstein. "That's the first time she didn't do what I told her."

They're strolling past the bars, peep shows and adult motels east of Cahuenga looking for a seedy location. Drackenstein points out a street sign altered by someone with white paint so it reads: HOL YWOOD B$^e$L$^{ie}$V$^e$D. "Let's use that," he says. Someone else, Crab notices as they get closer, has with chalk written an o in over the ie.

"She didn't want a kid Rod," Crab tells him, "yours or mine." Drackenstein stops talking and for a moment Crab thinks he's going to lapse into an uncharacteristic comraderie beyond business chat but Drackenstein starts grumbling that now the film is really behind schedule, that it's cost him a fortune and the whole project is starting to look like a bomb.

"I keep thinking of calling it off," he says, "but what the hell I'm already in personally for a couple of bucks, just because I believed in the project, what a mistake, that's where integrity gets you. Fucking zoo," he says, looking around.

Drackenstein stops to get a paper from a vending machine and does a double take at the front page.

TOPLESS BOTTOM WREAKS HAVOC. Barebreasted Actress Caught on Freeway Smoking Joint. Sex star Clover

Bottom was arrested this afternoon on the Golden State Freeway driving a late model Stingray nude to the waist and smoking a marijuana cigarette. In her wake a series of fender-benders backed up the Golden State from Los Feliz to the Pasadena interchange, as astonished motorists apparently lost control of their vehicles and of themselves at the sight of the buxom Bottom cruising by at 85 mph.

Word of Miss Bottom's ride quickly got around on CB radio and she was soon surrounded by a convoy of truckers jockeying for a better view and making it intentionally difficult for the CHP to pull her over. "She was exceeding the speed limit," said the arresting officer, who seemed a little shaken by the episode. "She was using an apparently unlawful substance when apprehended. She was in a condition of indecent exposure. And she is also charged with creating a traffic hazard."

Harley True, a teamster on his first haul through Los Angeles with a cargo of plastics from Corpus Christi to Bakersfield, commented that "this here Shaky City is sure everything they say." Miss Bottom, producer Rod Drackenstein's latest discovery, is playing the lead in his undoubtedly X-rated *Blown Away*, now in production.

Drackenstein is excited. "This is worth a million bucks," he says, "it's perfect, as if Plotz had made the whole thing up." There's a picture next to the article of Clover in a policeman's jacket hunched over with her hands clawing at her face.

Clover walks out of her trailer looking okay, but when the camera starts rolling and she opens her mouth to say her lines nothing comes out. Tears begin streaking her face. She lets her head fall, her chest is heaving and her lips are twitching out of control.

"Good," yells Drackenstein, "keep it rolling, get a closeup of her face." She stands there with the camera on her till Drackenstein is satisfied and tells the camera man to cut.

"Terrific footage," he says. "That was really fine," he puts his arm around Clover. He's elated. "You see, that's what we're reaching for. Spontaneity."

Clover is sobbing.

"What's the matter, baby? Come on, let's go back to the trailer for a little therapy," says Drackenstein.

"What am I, your scumbag?" says Clover.

"That's right," says Drackenstein. "Let it all hang out."

She lets him lead her back to the trailer. When they come out a half hour later her face looks hard. "Sorry guys, I'm cool now. There's nothing like giving head to clear your mind," she says, laughing.

Drackenstein coughs. "Well we still have this scene. Let's do it," he says. "Isn't that what Gary Gilmore said?" says Crab. Everybody else is too embarrassed to say anything.

"She gets off on humiliating herself," Crab tells Lazonga.

"Does giving head imply losing face?" Lazonga answers. "What she's getting off on is coke, there's a stash in the trailer," she adds.

"I know but it's extremely sad," says Crab.

"Not sad. Pathetic," says Lazonga. "The thin pathos of our sexual merry-go-round. The only thing to do is get off it."

"Or get it off," says Wang. "Or get it on."

Crab is still in love with her. It is not mellow. Overripe, maybe. It's been going on too long. He feels that something inside him is going to split open. Like a cocoon. Falling in love is not to make you happy, it occurs to Crab. That's not the point. Happiness is overrated, there are more important things than happiness, even in Southern California. Falling in love is a mode of self-destruction, he thinks. For the first time he understands the old connection between joy and insanity. Love and death. He feels he's in the hands of an ancient and pitiless deity, whoever or whatever it is. His hands shake more or less continuously and he has recurrent stomach cramps. He knows he's on the verge. It seems an odd passion in the California sunshine. He is not having a nice day. Everything is not all right. He is not okay. Crab is going to disappear, he thinks. His shell is broken. He's going into flux. Immersion. Drowning. Metamorphosis. What would re-emerge, if anything, he doesn't know. Something different, darker, deeper. He keeps thinking about the quake faults that seam Shaky City. The sense of its own impermanence that keeps it on the GlamourTram. The dynamism of flux.

Drackenstein is eating with Clover in a posh Chinese restaurant in Beverly Hills. Suddenly she glares at a man at the next table and says, in a loud voice, "Stop looking at my tits." Dead silence in the restaurant, Drackenstein saying something apologetic in the direction of the next table, something mollifying to Clover, Clover saying, in a loud voice, "No, I mean you, mister. Stop looking at my tits, they're my tits," titters in the restaurant, Drackenstein calling for the check, hustling her out, Clover saying, "Where we going, I'm tired of people wanting to fuck me."

Crab desperate. He would do anything to reassert his power over Clover. She's getting more demoralized every day. She's abandoned all her self improvement schemes. Lazonga has written her off. She's completely under Drackenstein's spell and even that isn't sustaining her. Crab decides on Wang's love potion, as a desperation measure. He's abandoned the realm of fatality for that of possibility. Things are clearly out of control, even Drackenstein's control. After all his efforts Crab has to admit he no longer knows what's happening, what has happened, or what is going to happen. He feels completely power-less, as if he doesn't exist. He's drowning in his own experience.

A hot dry Santa Ana blowing through the city causes a series of brush fires in the outskirts, clouds of black smoke on the horizon. Heat unrelenting, infernal. Everybody is in a bad mood. Drackenstein involved in a string of petty irritations. His car breaks down on the Santa Monica and he gets a ticket for leaving it on the side of the freeway. The lead on another project ODs and she's in the hospital for "exhaustion."

Drackenstein has never seen a production fall apart the way this one seems to be doing. He's suspicious of Crab. The snuff footage has disappeared, he assumes it was stolen. The cast and crew are unruly on the set and he even suspects someone of dropping drugs in the coffee urn. One day everybody is yawning and falling asleep, the next everyone is picking fights. Once the cast gets so horny they have to beat copulating actors out from behind the props between takes. Then there's the afternoon when everyone has the giggles, someone starts laughing at a purely routine remark, "Get the big dolly, will you Joe," and can't stop, it's contagious, two actors are incapacitated with stomach cramps brought on by belly laughs, makeup is ruined by actors teary with mirth, one girl has to go to the infirmary in uncontrollable spasms of giggling hiccups. Electronic equipment malfunctions at odd moments driving the technicians crazy. Scenes filmed of domestic interiors appear in rushes with Hima-layan mountains in the background, a love scene when the film is developed turns out to be pygmies hunting elephants followed by fragments of a Dodger game. The women suddenly get very angry about the sexual exploitation involved in the movie and Purdy Hicks, sexploitation starlet, dig it, draws up a petition demanding plot modification.

Drackenstein, against his better judgment, suspects Crab of

laying a curse on the production through some kind of psychic disruption on grounds it's destructive for Clover. He even goes to Lazonga for a reading.

"Beware of wasting money this week," she says. "This is a good time to reexamine things. Delay all projects. Wait and see." When he asks her to consult the crystal ball about his future she reports she sees "green paper rectangles disappearing down a dark hole. I see shiny golden dust blowing away in the wind. Does this mean anything to you?"

Drackenstein suspends filming for a week. The last straw is that Clover can't get her lines right, they'd do ten takes of a scene, she would forget her lines, they would make giant cue cards for her, then her timing would be off, he tries speeding her up with coke, slowing her down on downs, nothing works, nothing she does makes any sense, her feelings have no connection with what's going on around her. Drackenstein decides to put Clover in the hospital for "exhaustion" and finish the film with a stand-in. This girl is an absolute dead ringer for Clover, which isn't so strange since Clover is such a total Southern California type. And she couldn't possibly be a worse actress.

Immediate result of love potion would be frightful. Clover wanting to make love again and again and not being able to come. Finally Crab admitting he has given her a love potion, had hypnotized her from the beginning. "I don't believe in love potions Boris. Or in hypnosis. Fuck me goddamit, I feel like shit." Frenzy. Rage. Nymphomania. Depression.

Blond blond. California blond. Pampas grass blond. Corn silk blond. Haystack blond. Horse tail blond. Sun blond. Sperm blond. Sand blond. Bland blond. Leached blond. White blond. Bone china blond. Bleached bone blond. Ghostly blond. Movie screen blond.

Trembling in Crab's arms. Then suddenly calm, instead of angry, sad. "What are you crying about?" Crab asks. "Everything," seeming now filled with pity. For herself. Even for Drackenstein. For Crab. "Poor Boris. It's useless for sure. Your silver cat glow. I wanted to be your sad beautiful lady."

Wild dry wind raking city, smoke on horizon, infernally hot, evacuations ordered in the suburbs, Drackenstein in incredibly bad mood. Crab very low he knows when she disappears he disappears.

Drackenstein would be trying to catch up with the production schedule, the cast would have been working all day, scene after scene, Clover would be exhausted, this is the way it might happen, or she would have a hysterical fight with Crab or for the first time with Drackenstein, or both, or she couldn't get a scene right, it would be a love scene, Clover would be naked, Drackenstein would make her do it over and over again. "The hell with the money she's going to do it till she gets it right," it would be up in the hills, or in Griffith Park, infernally hot, "Try to get your real feelings into it," Drackenstein would keep telling her. She would insist on resting in the trailer instead of eating dinner, "Bring me back a ham sandwich."

They would have to break into the trailer, she would be on the cot naked, arms and legs spread, face relaxed, radiant, "We finally have our snuff scene," a technician might quip, "Get a shot," Drackenstein would murmur, the ambulance, the doctor trying to wake her up too late, "She took a whole pharmacopoeia, this place looks like a drugstore," police asking questions, reporters, "Do we tell them she ODed?" "Tell them," Drackenstein would say, thinking a minute, "that she's still alive, that they're trying to revive her, that she choked on a ham sandwich. For the sake of the fans."

Or, Plotz, himself, according to Plotz, would be the first to arrive at the scene, breaking the door down with the help of one of the grips, and would immediately recognize she's gone. He'd stagger out of the trailer where he'd meet Drackenstein who, noticing the look on his face, would ask, "Is Clover all right?" "No," Plotz would answer. "She's dead." Drackenstein would race past the mangled door, wild eyed when he sees Clover spread-eagled on the bed, would grab her, shake her, yell at her, "Talk to me Clover, say something. Please." Would call for a mirror and hold it up to her face to see if he can see her breath on it. Would scream at the paramedics to do something, would have to be restrained, would collapse in a corner. One of the paramedics would give him a hypodermic. "He finally cracked," Crab would say. "Like me."

Or, maybe she would last be seen boarding a private plane on a trip to Vegas in the company of a short man in a dark suit and dark glasses, but at the last minute this man would decide to meet her there later. He would give her a kiss and walking back to his chauffeured limo parked next to the private airstrip, look over his shoulder at her as she climbs on board.

LOS ANGELES (AP). We heard a loud crash and bits of skull, bits of flesh and a couple dozen chunks of the plane came showering down. Two very distinct bodies falling with their arms and legs twisting. Police and firemen said they had difficulty restraining the souvenir hunters who flocked to the area. They were carrying off everything from airplane parts to actual pieces of bodies. You couldn't believe it. We did our best to stop them, but quite a few must have got away with some part or other.

Fuchsia bougainvillea begonia mimosa jacaranda bottlebrush bird-of-paradise agapanthus eucalyptus yucca pampas grass red hot poker prickly pear jasmine hibiscus calla lily poinciana anthurium ice plant matalija poppy.

# II

# REVISION

"This is not finished," Plotz has himself saying in his manuscript.

"You've got a terrific concept going here," says Drackenstein. "You got everything in here but a happy ending and you know Miracle's going to want a happy ending."

"A happy ending, impossible. There's no cause and effect, it's implausible," says Plotz.

"No problem. We'll just bring her back to life," says Drackenstein.

"But I go into this in my manuscript," says Plotz in his manuscript. "Right here where you say, 'Miracle's going to want a happy ending,' and I go, 'A happy ending, impossible. There's no cause and effect, it's implausible,' says Plotz. 'No problem. We'll just bring her back to life,' says Drackenstein. 'But I go into this in my manuscript,' says Plotz in his manuscript. 'Right here where you say, —Miracle's going to want a happy ending. And I go, —A happy ending, impossible . . .'"

At that moment an implausible rumbling begins and the earth quakes under their feet and for a half a second before it stops they wonder when and if it's going to stop.

"Christ that felt like a six," says Plotz. "Why can't they predict these things?"

"Tilt," says Drackenstein. "Start over. Let's not lose our grip on reality. Remember, it's only a story. We'll just bring her back to life. The idea is everybody thinks she's dead and when she comes back it's like a miracle, there's a big reconciliation and she gets married. What they don't know is they're dealing with a stand-in, the show goes on, so in a larger sense she comes back to life."

"Anyway there's always the next one coming up. Monroe, Mansfield, it's all the same story," Plotz has himself saying in his manuscript. He can come up with brilliant story ideas but unfortunately is already dead at this point, of his final stroke of genius.

"I was talking to John Huston about this the other day," says Drackenstein. "He said it's the very nature of pictures to make the people on the screen heroic, even godlike. He said it's a kind of pantheism. He said they aren't flesh and blood, they're shadows of our own projection. Then he said something very striking, I can almost quote him, he said he's surprised there aren't more casualties among the gods, more people who are incapable of handling themselves under a whole new set of conditions such as occur when they're elevated into being sex objects and things like that, he said he'd think more of them would go off the deep end. Those were his very words. He should know."

"Anyway," says Plotz, "they keep coming. Remember how we played the original Bottom suicide for publicity, just before we started shooting *Pig*? Here's the article."

DEAD STAR LIVES. Clover Bottom, rumored dead last week in mysterious circumstances on location, turned up today at a news conference with her producer cheerful and smiling at reporters asking if she were the real Clover Bottom. "You never know what's going to happen next," said Rod Drackenstein when asked if it was all a hoax. "Life is a bad movie with an improbable plot."

Bottom, whose scandalous public behavior has been getting headlines, is about to start her first big role in Dracken-

stein's *My Little Pig*, a sex rated production about the girl
next door. *Pig*, Drackenstein claims, is wholesome pornog-
raphy suitable for the whole family. "Leave out the 'i' in *Pig*
and you get PG," Rod says with a wink. "It's all in a pig's i."
The eye of the beholder, no doubt.

"Yeah, we got a lot of press out of that one. There's still a
rumor circulating that she's her stand-in."

"It's true Clover is a different person now. Quieter," says
Plotz.

"But crazier," says Drackenstein. "And she's been slipping
lately. Her image is fading. She's dead in the media. I think it's
time for a public resurrection."

Drackenstein uses his political connections to get Clover, last
minute, into a big benefit in the Hollywood Bowl. That day
turns out to be like a revival of the sixties, Baez, Dylan, Timothy
Leary are on stage, Tom Hayden giving a speech, Jane Fonda is
there, Allen Ginsberg even reads a poem. The risk is that Clover
would be submerged, but what happens is that she does some
strange trick with the crowd, she doesn't do anything. She's
completely static. Maybe that's the bit, she just stands there not
doing anything she just stands there saying "Thank you, thank
you," while the crowd roars, whistles and applauds, it's mysterious, as if for some reason, certainly no reason she's aware of,
she's become the passive focus of a mass identity, appearing in a
short white tunic that exposes her breasts and most of her
buttocks, pure victim, it's almost eerie.

"What do these little zombies see in her?" asks Plotz.

"Maybe they get off on her tits," says Drackenstein.

"We're going to make a million dollars," says Miracle.

She comes off the stage glowing with energy. "You see, you

have to have faith is the trip. It happens now and then. All I need is five or ten thousand people paying attention to me and applauding wildly." She looks like she's just had an orgasm, like she's filled with some secret knowledge, like she's been broken open, ecstatic, like the corpse of a drowned woman Drackenstein once saw. He has the sudden feeling that if he doesn't bring her down she's going to fly off into outer space and never come back. He gets her into a big sweater and a pair of baggy pants, oversize shades, and hustles her out of there.

Where Drackenstein takes her is to see *My Little Pig*, on the theory that seeing the earlier film might help pull her together. There's a matinee at The Grot, a theater in a shopping center called Consumers World, landscaped in terraces of concrete and steel with decorative rectangles of water and patches of astroturf. They come in on the scene they did on location in Santa Ana where the mother nods out on pills leaving her young teenage daughter alone with the stepfather, who wants to tie her up and spank her. They'd found a shabby bungalow in an old subdivision that was perfect for that sort of seedy sequence, the mother saying, "You oughta try one of these reds, hon," flicking her cigarette in the wastebasket, and telling the daughter she ought to do what her daddy tells her. In the Grot as they watch the film, Drackenstein asks Clover if it reminds her of her life as a teenager. She says sort of but it doesn't seem real anymore. She says the movie doesn't seem real either. "Anyway I can't really tell the difference anymore, it blows me out. I want to leave."

They walk out of the darkness of The Grot into the dazzling sunlight of Consumers World, bright California sun on glittering concrete, Drackenstein has to blink till he can see. Zomboid shoppers in colorful polyesters slide through the mall on people movers. Muzak fills the mellow air. Jolly cement cartoon characters are placed here and there for children to play on, none are. Mays and Magnins and Montgomery Wards stretch low against the sky in vast blank white boxes.

"It's beautiful to be back in the world again," says Clover.

As he drives back with her from the film, Drackenstein realizes he's completely in love with Clover, and has been for some time. It's not mellow. Overripe, maybe. He feels that something inside him is going to split open. Falling in love is not to make you happy, it occurs to Drackenstein. That's not the point. Happiness is overrated, there are more important things than happiness, even in Southern California. Falling in love is a mode of self-destruction, he thinks. For the first time he understands the old connection between joy and insanity, love and death. He feels he's in the hands of an ancient and pitiless deity, whoever or whatever it is. He knows he's on the verge of breaking apart. He's going into flux, immersion, drowning. Metamorphosis. What will re-emerge if anything he doesn't know. Something different, darker, deeper. He's drowning in his own experience. His life is about to begin.

At the same time Clover is coming back to public life, Crab is disappearing from history, suspending animation at odd hours, going into catalepsy at Dennys and Der Wienerschnitzels. Metempsychotic, he tells his friends about mystic meetings with dogs and cats, all sorts of hallucinatory animals that Crab calls "other selves." He tells his friends of being approached by a dog at night in Laguna moonlight, a large dog of unknown breed, glowing with the light of its own intelligence, waiting for an answer. I'm Ccrab and I'm Crab. I'm concerned with power and I'm concerned with knowledge. The power dog, the cat knowledge, the reincarnations of sudden memory. Clifton's and Coffee Dan's, Utter McKinley undertaker sign of Los Angeles thirty years ago. The calm strength from watching a self peel off and die into the black cosmic wind like an autumn leaf.

When Clover and Drackenstein get back to the Dracken-schloss there's a letter for Clover from Crab, who's dropped out of sight, in which Plotz has Crab predicting Plotz's own death. Clover reads it and hands it to Drackenstein without comment. "Dear Clover, Good night, this is a note of withdrawal and adieu, withdrawal not only from the 'brave new world' you find yourself stranded in, I've lost my yen for new worlds, there are no new worlds, the future is over, destiny is doom, it is written, it is overwritten, contained in the book of eternity, when the future is known it is no longer the future, so what good is a fortune teller, for some time now I've been fading, split in two, each half a facsimile of my self, whoever that is, and now I, using the pronoun loosely, I find fragmentation has become progres-sive, till I don't know how many there are of me, I find I'm one person with you, another with Drackenstein, I'm overcommit-ted, stretched too thin, reduced to the status of a series of ghosts gliding about to no effect, I am now many people, or part of many people, there comes a time when it no longer makes any sense to try to have an effect on the world, when we must retreat to our source, our vital essence, even at the expense of individual identity and despite the pain of separation, fear of ego death, torn from mother's breast, earth pulled from under feet, it's beyond imagination, nothing to do but take the plunge, plunge ahead, tomorrow Drackenstein goes to visit Plotz and finds police cars in front of the door, he races in and discovers Plotz shot by his ex-wife, his body still there in the patio, his ex-wife sobbing in the living room, Drackenstein gets into a fight with Miracle over who's finishing the script, Clover sleeps with Roy, years later she's running an acting school, Plotz's manu-

script is published as *Blown Away*, Drackenstein is tormented
by his sick daughter, he's in love with Clover who now visits
Miracle in his office every day for lunch, later Miracle is also
screwing Drackenstein's daughter, Drackenstein gets out of the
movie business, he goes into therapy with Roxoff, he's sued by
his ex-wife, he's arrested for exposing himself on an airplane, he
develops eye trouble, becomes a psychic, years later he's teaching
psychic healing in a Free School in Boulder, Colorado, his daughter is a famous actress, Crab goes blind and disappears, I used to
be Crab, an expedition establishes beyond doubt the reality of
Atlantis in the area of the Bermuda Triangle, a series of six
plagues including warts and crickets sweeps the continent, a
man named Sneath discovers a way of growing many crops on
one plant and this revolutionizes world agriculture, an unprece-
dented yo-yo fad captivates the free world, a twelve-year-old
math genius formulates a quadrilateral triangle and opens the
way for research into the fourth dimension, genetic experiments
solve the dog feces problem by developing 'clean' dogs whose
waste can be used as fuel in the form of briquettes, similar
experiments produce vampires and dragons, men with horns
come out of northern Turkistan, yours truly, B. O. Crab."

In the book you're reading it all turns out the way Crab
predicts. Drackenstein goes to see Plotz the next day, mostly
because he reads Crab's letter. He does in fact find police in
front of the door, Plotz dead, his ex-wife being questioned by the
police. Drackenstein's remaining faith in the futurity of the
future crumbles, along with his morale. When he calls Miracle
to cancel the scheduled script conference, Miracle says he wants
his technical advisor, Philitis, to go over what they have, Drackenstein says he wants to finish it up himself based on Plotz's
renovelization, he knows the material, it's his story, Miracle tells

him to read the contract, Drackenstein says he doesn't care about the contract, he knows the film, he doesn't want an outsider who doesn't understand the conception to screw up the story, Miracle says all right, "we'll take a meeting. With my boy Philitis," Friday two o'clock at United International.

Drackenstein occupies himself with arrangements concerning the denouement of Plotz. He calls Malinow and Silverman Mortuary and arranges a service at Eden Memorial Park Chapel. He discovers some nieces and nephews in the east. He composes a death notice for the *Times*. On that day, Tuesday, October 24, 1978, the weather is hot, around ninety. In the book you're reading a xerox of part of a page of the L.A. *Times* for that date is included on page 167. Drackenstein suddenly feels like taking off down Wilshire Boulevard all the way to Santa Monica and the beach, he hasn't done it for years. The city is ringed by fires, fanned by the Santa Ana, the devilwind, which, though now dying, has already swept flames as high as a hundred feet through many areas around Los Angeles, destroying more than eighty houses so far, he wonders if anyone he knows got hit in the Malibu fire burning through Broad Beach right down to the ocean. Or the one in Pacific Heights, you could see the smoke over there, black and ominous, evacuees are being sheltered at Brentwood High. The smoke reminds him of black crepe, reminds him of Plotz, he keeps thinking Utter McKinley, a mortuary that for years had a huge sign up in Hollywood to remind people on the GlamourTram where they're all heading. The *Times* horoscope says he should "find ways to gain more abundance in the future. 4a," must be a typo. For a cheap bitch who's learned how to sell her trick to the highest bidder, or a sacrificial victim to the system of which he's an increasingly marginal part? One thing certain is that she doesn't have any better idea

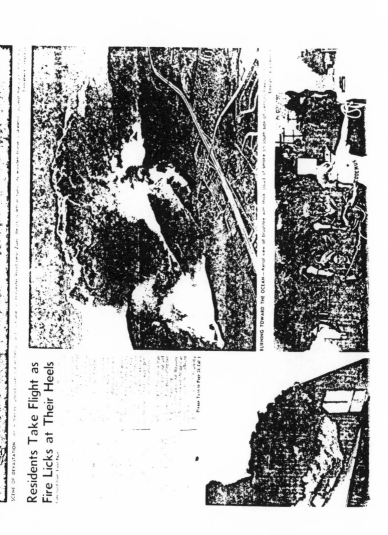

SCENE OF DEVASTATION

## Residents Take Flight as
## Fire Licks at Their Heels

Please Turn to Page 2A, Col 1

BURNING TOWARD THE OCEAN—Aerial view of brushfire air thick cloud of smoke on south side of

of her identity than anyone else, why should she, it would only get in the way. Her horoscope advises her to make time for personal affairs later in the day. "Follow the advice of experts." That's what she's doing, of course, with Miracle her new producer and a new agent and her lawyer and someone writing promo exclusively for her, she doesn't need to think, or even act, all she needs to do is exist. He might try to make an appointment with her for later in the day, if she's not busy with Miracle. The two have much in common, Miracle could be running a chain of hardware stores or a multinational conglomerate, he has no opinion, takes no stands, believes nothing, he processes things like a computer, like Clover he's empty, ready for anything.

Meanwhile in the book you're reading the Sheriff investigates the origin of the fires, believed to be arson according to the late edition of the *Times*, which hasn't yet picked up the story about Plotz, but notes that Sid Vicious slashes his wrists, Gig Young shoots himself and his wife of three weeks, Sal Mineo's killer is soon to stand trial, Keith Richards is convicted of heroin possession, and Maya Plisetskaya is sick. No doubt Plotz is to be cited in tomorrow's casualty list. On the other hand, Governor Brown's appearance at a Wilmington union hall is covered by eight TV crews and his debate with Evelle Younger holds viewer interest throughout, while Mike Curb, candidate for lieutenant governor and former president of MGM Records, denies being involved in the production of a pornographic motion picture, the candidate for attorney general has image problems, and a movie stunt woman is half way up El Capitan in Yosemite where a team of three expert rock climbers recently fell to their deaths, in a solo attempt to climb the monolith, expected to take eight to ten days. From 1,500 feet below, watchers "could see the sunlight glinting off a gold ring in her left ear." Drackenstein calls Clover to see if she wants to go see *Zoot Suit* tonight, a play resulting from the collaboration of Gordon Davidson and Luis Valdez of El Teatro Campesino, but she's already going with Roy. Of course.

It turns out that Plotz has no cemetery reservation in the book you're reading, and this is holding up the funeral. Drackenstein answers an ad for a plot in the *Times*: "good location, murmuring trees, moving, must sell. $450 or best offer." He concludes the deal, for cash, in a Hamburger Hamlet in West Hollywood, with a curious little man who advises him against cremation. "There's nothing like a good plot," he tells Drackenstein. "You put the body in, you cover it with six feet of real estate, you know what you got. No surprises. You ever got to check up on something you can always dig it up. With cremation what have you got? Ashes. You sneeze at the wrong time it could all blow away." By the time they get around to the funeral the weather cools off. Clover is there, Wang, a few friends. It's in a walled gothic garden, shrubs and trees tossing in a damp wind, a sky full of scurrying black clouds and mist veiling the mountains. It's just the way Plotz would have written it. Corny.

On the way back from the funeral Drackenstein picks up strange vibes from Clover. He knows something is up, he can practically read her mind. When they get back home he invites her out on the deck and asks her what's happening. The only answer he gets is a pair of mockingbirds singing to one another in the tree tops. When she finally speaks all she does is repeat the word happening with a question mark after it. Drackenstein tells her to stop playing innocent. It gives her a guilty look he tells her.

"I don't have to answer your questions," she tells him. Now

it's Drackenstein's turn to be silent. The victim becomes the executioner, he muses. The girl he shapes and uses, then falls in love with, becomes in this version of the plot the agent of destruction. Finally Drackenstein says, "It's Roy, right?"

She gives a little nod. It seems while they're lounging around the pool in their swimsuits Roy and Clover decide to undertake a trial of chastity by playing a game of nude chess. They fail the test. Something about news of Plotz's death breaking down their discipline. Clover is contrite. "Okay I'm real sorry," she says. "I won't do it again. Really, Rod. You have to see it from Roy's point of view. He feels like you put him down. He thinks you adopted him because of phony liberal attitudes. He says he was better off left with his people. He's just trying to make some kind of identity for himself."

"The only kind of identity Roy is going to get out of screwing his father's women, and this isn't the first time he's done it, is mother fucker. And besides how can you do that the day Plotz got blown away?"

"That doesn't say anything about the way I felt about Victor, Rod. I really liked Victor. I even made love with him once. Just once," she adds quickly. "Because he wanted to so much."

"Because he wanted to so much," Drackenstein repeats the words, "do you realize how busy you're going to get if you maintain that criterion?"

"What does criterion mean?" she answers.

He goes to the phone and calls the Chateau Marmont for a reservation, he decides he wants to get out of the house for a while.

In the book you're reading Drackenstein winds slowly down the canyon in the yellow Stingray. The license plate on the white Mercedes ahead of him is U R DUNN, he supposes it's the name of the owner. He tunes in some mellow rock and passes a slow-moving Chevy van painted with a wave motif carrying two surfboards on a rack, with a plate that says YYY TRI. A little later he's passed by a vintage red Cadillac convertible in super condition with double tail like a jet fighter and plate that says FINS. What, he wonders, is trying to tell him what. He comes out of the mouth of Laurel Canyon and cuts over to the Chateau Marmont, the neon sign on the roof already lit, the sun fallen behind the hills, the hotel's vaguely gothic outline looming against a layer of orange between olive hills and the descending purple, flanked by masses of low evergreens and tasselled with long-stemmed palms. The moment has the easy thrill of a postcard, dear Cathy June, wish you were here.

That night sitting in his room in the book you're reading, the glittering bowl of Los Angeles through his window at the Marmont, Drackenstein already knows what will happen at his meeting with Miracle Friday.

"You call this a happy ending?" says Miracle.

"It's a happier ending," says Drackenstein.

"This is Plotz's version of the end?" asks Philitis. Philitis has given up his tweeds for an Italian suit, narrow tie, Rolex watch.

"Plotz never got around to finishing an ending," says Drackenstein.

"The whole conception of the fortune teller as prophet of doom is too gloomy," says Miracle.

"And he's not believable as a psychic," says Philitis. "He's as psychic as my asshole."

"I've never met a psychic asshole before," says Drackenstein. "Look, I'll stake my career on the idea of the psychic."

"What career?" says Philitis.

"It's fake," says Miracle. "People will not buy it. Don't get me wrong. I have nothing against the fake as long as it's the real thing. What people are willing to pay for. That's the kind of prophet we're interested in, Rod. Profit and loss. A fortune teller is someone who counts his fortune. This ending is not happy enough. I believe in really happy endings, it's a matter of faith. Happy endings are my religion, you might say."

"The trouble with Philitis' suggestions," says Drackenstein, "is they demonstrate his lack of taste."

"I hope so," says Miracle. "I worked with him for months to get rid of it. At least he's got a bankable concept, the adventures of a sex goddess."

"What I want to know is who's going to play Mandy now?" says Philitis in the book you're reading. "Clover can't do it because she's either pregnant or dead, or because she's in the hospital for exhaustion."

"No problem," says Drackenstein. "We'll find a look-alike."

"What about your daughter, Rod?" says Miracle. "She looks like a look-alike."

"No. Impossible."

"Nothing's impossible," says Miracle. "Think big, Rod. Most people move from the complex of possibility to the simplicity of fate, but our business is to reverse the process. That's why they call this the city of dreams."

"That's why it's a city with no past and no future," says Drackenstein.

"Try being an optimist for once," says Miracle. "It's more patriotic."

In his room at the Marmont, Drackenstein can see Plotz waking up one morning in the book you're reading, and the details of life are incandescent down to the utmost trivia, loose hair, bottle caps, toenails, old tin cans, seashells, fresh baloney.

The sky is blue for once and he walks out the door to the patio into a warm breeze bringing the rattle of dusty palms and the smell of star jasmine. For the first time he can remember he thinks about where he's living, redwood decks hummingbird feeders swimming pools wild prickly pear whale spouts tar pits avocado pits citrus smell neon sunsets over Catalina subdivision flags crackling in hot wind chili dogs catpiss-juniper sage-stained air of chaparral-canyons late at night boats bobbing in Balboa Bay bright bellied spinnakers booming bright cars tacky parks freeways seashells and old tin cans and bottle caps and broken tiles in Rodia's Coney Island towers. A happy enchantment fills the air like light, is light, here, beyond language, where only one ending is possible and it's not a happy one. This afternoon he has an appointment to have lunch with Nin and talk with Miller about his manuscript, an appointment that might change his life. His ex-wife, who he hasn't seen for years, walks into the patio, a twenty-two in her purse.

In the book you're reading, Drackenstein, sitting in his room, can now predict them shooting the new ending out of sequence from a script conceived by Miracle in which all parties are reconciled and are about to live happily ever after. On location in Avalon, a flowery patio overlooking the ocean where an occasional whale spouts and sounds. Drackenstein's daughter, Miranda, plays Mandy in the remaining scenes, Clover being either dead, pregnant or in the hospital for "exhaustion." Drackenstein himself is no longer in the project, and the gossip columns say he's leaving his production company, giving up control, leaving the industry, giving up. "Rod Drackenstein's career," he can see the *Herald Examiner* column, "can be summed up in one word—over."

In the book you're reading Drackenstein in the Chateau Mar-

mont already knows how the nondescript wooden door opens in
the book you're reading into a never-never land of ferns and
succulents, palmettos, pink petunias and fuchsias, white bego-
nias, vermilion impatiens, gold hibiscus, along a path through
low dunes to the white Malibu sand where she stands in jeans
and white t-shirt holding the baby and smiling at him. The
going rumor is she dropped Miracle for Elmer Perkin after
getting a bundle for child support. They go into the house, a lot
of wicker and bamboo, cushy sofas, a glass table on cinder blocks
on an enormous Persian rug, a look of ongoing improvisation,
brilliant afternoon sun leveling in over the ocean. "It's so good
living far away from Hollywood and Beverly Hills. I actually
have neighbors who aren't in show biz. Doctors, lawyers, rock
stars, writers." "What did you name it?" "This is Oscar Miracle
Bottom," leaning back against a Navaho rug in a corner filled
with orchid plants and African violets under a huge canvas
reminiscent of Monet's water lilies framed on one end by a
floor to ceiling ficus and a small Lipchitz on the other. Two cats
sleep curled up together on the rug. A Mozart aria is just audible
over the sound of surf, a kind of muzak. "Yes I got tired of being
a walking cunt. I've been studying. When I go back I'm taking
nothing but serious roles. I may even try theater. My agent is
talking to Davidson. Loretta." A woman murmuring in a West
Indian accent comes and takes the baby. "Why didn't you marry
Miracle?" "He's too old. In ten years he might not be able to do
it." "Wasn't he hurt when you got rid of him?" "In this town a
lot of people get hurt. That's the way it is. If you don't like the
action you get off the merry-go-round." "You sound committed." "I don't know about committed. I mean people I know
aren't even committed to their own personalities much less

their careers. If they're committed to anything it's changing themselves. For the better, of course." "You've changed." "I hope so. In those days I couldn't even remember who I was in bed with. And it was preferable that way." "What do you want to do?" "We could fly up to Mammoth. I'm learning how to ski." "Is there snow yet?" "I guess not. There's a play on Broadway I want to see." "It's three o'clock. The time change is the wrong way." "Do you want to go dancing?" "Is the Daisy open tonight?" "You're really out of touch Rod. Try Chez Moi. 274-8739." He goes to the phone and dials the number, noticing an open book on the table, Fitzgerald's unfinished novel, *The Last Tycoon*. "Your house has an unfinished look I admire. It reminds me of the unfinished house in the book you're reading," it says in the book you're reading.

Now in the book you're reading Drackenstein in his room sees himself keeping the appointment Plotz never got to keep with Henry Miller and Anais Nin, an appointment that might have changed his life. An appointment for lunch at Nin's Lloyd Wright house above Silver Lake, always a little like an invitation to the Acropolis. Drackenstein imagines seating himself, Henry not yet there, so he can look at the gorgeous Varda collage at the end of that splendid room overlooking patio, pool and hills, drawn into Anais' fine web, as one always is, with the sense that you have at last arrived at whatever you started looking for as a kid ripping yourself from the breast of your mediocre suburb or miscellaneous subdivision of sprawl city. Miller arrives with a genial apology for being late because he's been visiting a friend who's just had a double mastectomy, saying he's as hungry as a shark and musing that he's never fucked a woman with no tits, years of fury with him knifing in Anais' eyes. To avoid blood

Drackenstein might ask quickly, something, no matter what, whether his ideas about literature are any different now than they were in the old days.

"First of all," Miller says, "there's no such thing as literature. What most people call literature is just fossilized morality, don't you know. I prefer to talk about books, that seems more honest, and in any case there comes a time when you want to get out of the book too, do you see. Like that manuscript Plotz sent me. I would have told him not to try and finish it. The book was okay the way it was. Most books are too finished. They're claustrophobic."

"Do you reject books these days?" Drackenstein imagines himself asking.

"I don't reject anything, I don't reject anything. Books have the power to devalue and revalue your experience, just like money, don't you see. Sometimes you don't give a flying fuck about it and sometimes you're ready to lie, kiss ass or go out into the street with a tin cup."

Drackenstein might tell him how he lived at Place Clichy some years after Miller died, and remind him of Rue Caulincourt and the bridge over the cemetery, the walk from Clichy to La Fourche.

"Yes, yes, of course," Miller might say a little dreamily. "All that. Is Wepler still there?"

"Still there but expensive. And the waiters are old."

"Certainly," Drackenstein can imagine Miller telling him. "It could've all happened tomorrow. And to someone else as well as me."

"By an odd coincidence," Anais says, "I wanted to read you something Saul Bellow translated from Isaac Bashevis Singer. 'I wandered over the land and good people did not neglect me.

After many years I became old and white. I heard a great deal, many lies and falsehoods, but the longer I lived the more I understood that there were really no lies. Whatever doesn't really happen is dreamed at night. It happens to one if it doesn't happen to another, tomorrow if not today, or a century hence if not next year. What difference can it make? Often I heard tales of which I said, 'Now this is a thing that cannot happen.' But before a year had elapsed I heard that it actually came to pass somewhere.' I thought that would please you. It's from 'Gimpel the Fool.' "

"Of course," Henry says, "but life is not a book, don't you see. If everything that's going to happen is already written it makes a rotten story, a story it's up to us to unwrite. And from another point of view everything is unpredictable, and even when I wipe my nose, that's something that never happened before and nobody could have thought up ahead of time."